The Tall Ship Shakedown

The Tall Ship Shakedown

Neil S. Wilson

Tyndale House Publishers, Inc.
Wheaton, Illinois

Books in the Choice Adventures series

Library of Congress Cataloging-in-Publication Data

Wilson, Neil S., date
    The tall ship shakedown / Neil S. Wilson.
        p.   cm. — (Choice adventures ; #9)
    Summary: The reader's choices control the action as a group of Christian friends have adventures aboard a Coast Guard vessel during their spring break.
    ISBN 0-8423-5046-2
    1. Plot-your-own stories. [1. United States. Coast Guard—Fiction.
2. Adventure and adventurers—Fiction. 3. Christian life—Fiction.
4. Plot-your-own stories.] I. Title. II. Series.
PZ7.W69747Tal   1992
[Fic]—dc20   92-30500

Printed in the United States of America

99   98   97   96   95   94   93
 9   8   7   6   5   4   3   2   1

To Mom and Dad Wilson,
  Who love me
  Who read to me
  Who taught me to read
  Who taught me to love reading
  Missionaries in Brazil before the Whiteheads

  They've had part of the real adventure!

Willy looked out his second-floor apartment window past the icicles at the half-frozen lawn and shivered. "Isn't spring break ever gonna come?" he mumbled. Easter break from school was still a week away. It seemed like forever. The unexpected and unusual "winter" storm didn't help matters. He carefully leaned against the window and felt the cold seep through to his forehead.

The warm air from his mouth clouded the glass. He drew a line through the fog with his finger and pressed his face against the pane, trying to write his name with his nose. His eyes were crossed in concentration when suddenly—"Hey!" He waved frantically at a lone figure down below.

The figure waved back, bundled for cold and covered with the snow he was playing in. It was Chris, one of his best friends, who lived downstairs.

"You wanna come in?" yelled Willy.

He could barely hear Chris's shout. "No, come on out!"

Willy pointed in the direction of the apartment's main entrance. "Meet me!" he shouted. But on his way down the hall, another idea came to him. Instead of heading toward the main entrance, he turned around and snuck out the back. He raced around the side of the building, making fresh tracks in the new snow. Behind the evergreen at the corner of the building, Willy paused long enough to see

2

that Chris was waiting patiently out front, stamping the sticky snow from his shoes. Quickly grabbing enough snow for a huge ball, Willy attacked. Chris didn't know what hit him until it hit him. The snow globe landed right on top of his head, showering him and cascading down past his ears and into his collar. "Gotcha!" Willy yelled.

"Oh, yeah?" yelled Chris as he met Willy's rush with a tackle that carried Willy over backward into a snowdrift along the building. A brief but icy-cold wrestling match took place which they both lost when more snow decided at that moment to avalanche off the roof and cover them completely.

It was also at this moment that Willy realized he had forgotten to put on his boots before coming outside. All he had on were socks and shoes, which were now soaked. Spitting snow from his mouth as he struggled to his feet, he yelled, "Truce, truce! Let's get inside. I can't feel my toes anymore!"

In a second they were inside, brushing the last bits of snow off each other while they stood in the entryway.

"You've got a glacier in your collar, there, Chris," said Willy as he dug the snow out from behind Chris's neck. The two had known each other since the fourth grade, when Willy's family moved into the apartment above Chris and his mom.

Maybe it was the word *glacier,* but something got both boys thinking about school.

"Hey, how's your project coming for history?" asked Chris as they headed up the stairs to Willy's apartment.

"It's real cool," said Willy. "In fact, I was just about to work on it when you forced me to ambush you."

"*Work* on it? You mean you haven't been thinking about spring break?"

"No no no, you gotta see my project. It's radical!"

"Are you kidding? This is *snowball* weather! Come on, let's go back out and start a fight. Me against you, to the death."

Willy opened the door to the apartment and the two went inside. "No, c'mon, you gotta see this. Maybe you can even help me with it! C'mere, C'mere," Willy said, motioning excitedly toward his room.

Chris was getting irritated. Doing schoolwork when spring break was only a week away?

CHOICE ⇛

If Chris decides to follow Willy, turn to page 68.

If he tries to change Willy's mind, turn to page 94.

4

The Ringers thought it would be awesome to ride on a tall ship, so they decided to go to New London for the shakedown of the *Eagle*.

But what a week of waiting there was! Because of all the excitement of their upcoming spring break, the next week of school was agony! All the rushing around finding canvas duffels and packing made the days go only *slightly* faster. But finally, Saturday arrived.

Lee had arranged to meet the gang in front of the church at 8:00 A.M. sharp. Willy, who had been completely packed by Tuesday night, was there before 7:30. His friends weren't far behind. They quickly discovered that seven stuffed duffel bags made a great combination easy chair/deep dish wrestling pad. Bags and bodies were flying when Lee drove up in the Coast Guard van. With him was another recruiter named Ruth Ann.

After introducing Ruth Ann to each of the Ringers, Lee said, "The two of us will be your leaders during the next week. Now listen, we've got a long day ahead of us because we'll be driving straight through to New London. So . . . all aboard and we're history!"

It did turn out to be a long day. Traffic didn't help matters, and neither did a flat tire just outside New Haven. It was dark by the time the gang pulled into the Coast Guard Academy in New London. Everyone was tired and a little cranky. Lee and Ruth Ann bundled them off to bed in dormitories, and before they knew it, they awoke to Sunday morning bells. The churches in New London were ringing in the Lord's day!

Willy sat up in bed and yawned. "Where am I?" he asked. "Did I miss my turn to ring the bell at church?" His answer came in the form of four pillows smacking into him, one after the other. "You know what this means?" he yelled.

But before a war could break out, Willy noticed something at the end of his bed. Over the footboard was laid a brand new T-shirt. On the back were printed the words *"Eagle* crew"; on the front he found his name. Each of the other boys found an identical shirt on his footboard. (Well, OK, each boy had his own name on his shirt.) "I wonder what kind of ship the *Eagle* is," Willy wondered out loud.

"Whatever it is, these shirts are *cool!"* said Sam.

"Way cool," corrected Willy as he got up from his bed.

"No," said a voice from the doorway. "Those are for when it's hot; these are for when it's cool!" It was Lee, carrying five nylon jackets with *"Eagle"* on the back. He tossed one to each of the boys and told them to hurry and get dressed so they could make it to chapel on time. After a quick breakfast, at which they were joined by Jill, Tina, and Ruth Ann, the Ringers found themselves in a worship service with several hundred Coast Guard cadets.

Willy, who was sitting on the other side of Lee from Sam, leaned over and whispered, "Sam, it's really different going to church without any old people around."

6

Sam glanced up at Lee and whispered back, "I guess Lee is as old as we get!" Lee gave him a playful scowl.

During the worship service, the kids were impressed by the strong singing. They also enjoyed the chaplain's telling of the story of when Jesus was out on the Sea of Galilee with his disciples and fell asleep during a storm. The disciples were worried about sinking, but Jesus was taking a nap. When the disciples woke him in a panic, he simply spoke to the winds and waves and they became still. The chaplain reminded all of them that men and women who live on the seas eventually see some of the most powerful forces of nature at work. "When we see what the winds and the waves can do we will be afraid also," said the chaplain. "But we must remember that there is someone we can know who has power over every power. He has control over the forces of nature. While you are on land, and when you go to sea, make sure you take Jesus with you, all the way. He's the best traveling companion you could ever find!"

After leaving the chapel, Lee gathered the Ringers around Ruth Ann and himself. "Lunch is in about an hour, and cast off is shortly after," he announced. "Do you want to tour the *Eagle* now before we eat, or wait 'til after lunch?"

"Let's do it it now! I want to see the ship!" Chris was really anxious.

"No, let's wait until after lunch," Pete jumped in. He wanted plenty of time to see all the radar equipment on the ship.

Lee interrupted the discussion. "If it helps your decision at all, we'll be having lunch with the rest of the crew on board the ship."

"How about if we let Willy decide?" said Jim. "After all, if it wasn't for him seeing Lee on career day, we wouldn't be here."

What will Willy decide?

CHOICE ➤

If Willy decides to see the ship right away, turn to page 114.

If he waits until after lunch, turn to page 102.

8

Willy, *think:* Chocolate, vanilla, fudge, bananas, whipped cream, swirly stuff . . . Olympic ice cream champion Betty Metz performing live," said Chris.

"I know, but this is—"

"Willy? Turn down ice cream?" said Jill with disbelief.

"Not possible," added Jim.

"Willy, I'll help you finish the boat later. Come on."

"Boat?" asked Jim.

"Shi-*pp*. Shi-*pp*," corrected Willy, leaning in Chris's face.

Chris tried to ignore him, mumbling to the others, "It's just a model."

"It is not *just* a model," said Willy, wild-eyed. "It's a completely cool, delicate, ultra—"

"OK, OK," surrendered Chris, who now had his coat on and was standing in the doorway. He put his right hand partway inside the front of the coat, doing what he thought was an imitation of a British diplomat. "Dr. Peppah," he began in a mock-serious tone (referring to Willy's half of the nickname they shared at school), "could we pawssibly trouble you to take a recess from your most impawtant historical research to . . . " Chris couldn't keep up his little spoof any longer—"come stuff your face with *ic-c-ce cr-r-r-e-e-am?*"

Willy couldn't help but laugh. "You promise to help me finish it?"

Chris nodded.

"Well, when you put it that way—" Willy imitated Chris's fake dignified posture and extended his hand—"I accept your swell offer, sir." As he grabbed his coat and they headed out the door, he added, "I guess I was hungry anyway."

Most of the Ringers were already at the Freeze that afternoon. As Jill, Jim, Willy, and Chris burst through the door, a general shout of welcomes came from a booth and table toward the back. Chris thought to himself how interesting it was that such different kids could be such good friends.

Each of the kids around the table even had their own way of saying hello.

Sam, for instance, the shortest of the gang, jumped up from his seat and bowed. He smiled at Jill and said, "Señorita Jill, please sit in my chair. I would be honored and happy to sit on zee floor!"

Jill, blushing, tried to match Sam's playfulness. "Why, thank you so much, kind sir! But you don't have to sit on the floor. Just find another chair."

Pete, who had been sitting next to Sam, reached out and poked him. "But don't even think of taking my chair," he said.

Sam looked at Willy as if to say, "May I take your chair?" right after Willy sat down. "Touch my chair and you're hamburger," said Willy. Sam stayed standing. These guys were true friends.

Pete turned to the foursome who had just come in and said, "It's about time you guys got here. We thought Jim and Jill would be able to kidnap you in a flash."

"Well, it wasn't such an easy job," said Jim, laughing. "Willy was so interested in his school project that he almost turned down ice cream!"

"What was he doing it on? The chemical analysis of ice-cream toppings?" jibed Sam.

"Hey," said Willy in mock self-defense. "I was busy with serious historical research!"

Everyone laughed, but Chris added, "He's right, guys. Willy's building a boat in a—I mean *ship* in a bottle for his history project."

"What a great idea," said Sam. "When can I see it?" The others chorused their agreement with Sam.

"You guys can come back to my place in a while and I'll show it to you," said Willy. "I really can't stay long."

Right then, in walked an old gentleman who walked with a bounce in his step, like a kid. Like a well-trained choir, the Ringers said in one voice, "Hi, Pastor Whitehead!"

"Wonderful! You people are just the crew I'm looking for!" said the beaming grandfather, who *was* actually Jim and Tina's grandfather, and pastor of the Capitol Community Church, where the Ringers first started.

"What kind of crew do you need, Grandpa?" asked Jim.

"I need some help with a little drama tomorrow in church. I'm preaching about the time the apostle Paul lived through a shipwreck, and I thought the people might understand better if we acted out part of the story for them," said Pastor Whitehead.

"So when you said 'crew,' you really meant *crew,* huh?" said Tina, smiling. Everyone nodded and said that it would be fun. Everyone, that is, except Willy. He was still thinking about getting his project finished.

CHOICE

If Willy goes along with the others, turn to page 88.

Earlier Chris tried to talk Willy out of working on his project. If he decides to support Willy this time, turn to page 28.

Lee sensed that Sam was hesitating. He decided to make a guess. "Sam, do you know how to swim?"

There was no sense in hiding it. "Well," Sam said, "I guess I've never tried."

"That's fine," said Lee. "In fact, it will help us in training. People often get in trouble in survival situations because they can't swim. We can help you start learning if you like, but we'll also make sure that you know how to use your life vest correctly, so that swimming won't be necessary, OK?"

"OK." Sam felt relieved. *This guy is really all right!*

After they finished breakfast, the kids were taken out on deck and issued special harnesses to go with their life vests. Seaman Marley was their teacher. "You won't have to wear these all the time, squirts. But if we get into a storm and I catch one of you without your harness there's gonna be big trouble! Do I make myself clear?"

"Yes," murmured the kids.

"I didn't hear you!" shouted the huge sailor, scowling.

"Yes, sir!" they said loudly, in unison.

Marley smiled with satisfaction. "Not bad, squirts! We may make sailors out of you yet! Now, in stormy weather, we want you to attach your harness to the lines we will have strung up around the ship. If a wave sweeps over the deck and you lose your footing, the lines and harness will keep you with us. If you should fall overboard, we'll throw you a line with a clip on the end to attach to your harness. As you can see, your harness is your friend!"

Next, Marley showed the kids one of the survival rafts they would be using in training. It came in a sealed container that held the raft, paddles, and basic survival gear. He explained how the raft inflated automatically when a certain valve was turned. The valve operated a small cylinder of pressurized gas attached to the raft. He had Jim open the valve, and they all stood back and watched the oversized rubber donut spring to life.

Marley explained that the raft and equipment were designed for four people. He also unpacked the survival gear and showed the kids how to use each item.

He had just shown them how to stow the paddles in the raft when a gust of wind swept across the deck and lifted the raft like a feather. It went over the edge of the ship and into the water. It landed, right side up, next to the *Hawk*.

Marley calmly walked over to the railing and looked down. "Well, it wasn't exactly my plan, but it'll work." Turning back to the Ringers, he said, "I need two volunteers . . . Jim and Willy! You will now demonstrate how the harnesses work. Step this way."

As Jim and Willy came toward him, he picked up a rope that had a clip on the end of it. He attached the clip to Jim's harness and explained that he was about to lower Jim down into the raft. "It's very simple: you trust me," he said.

Jim climbed over the railing and stood on the outside, with his feet on the deck, white knuckles holding the railing.

14

Marley said, "Son, look at me. Do I look like I will have any trouble holding your weight? Now, I just want you to let go and walk backwards down the side of this ship."

Jim tried to think of something funny to say, but he was too scared to think.

So he let go. . . .

Turn to page 38.

Pete slipped the headphones on, found the power button, and pressed it. Nothing happened.

Next to him, Jill cleared her throat. She reached down behind the receiver and plugged it into a receptacle on the wall. "Don't mind me, Pete," she said with a really sweet smile. "But I've got the basic connections down."

Pete chuckled. He knew about electronic gadgets, but Jill had a real knack for electrical appliances.

Immediately, the headphones began to talk to Pete. The sailor called the Coast Guard base to find out if there was a record of a satellite distress code for the *Marlin*. Sure enough, there was. Pete punched the code into the receiver keyboard and pressed the send button. His heart beat exactly twice, and then a loud single beep sounded in his ear. Five seconds later, another beep sounded. Pete practically yelled, "I've got them. I don't know how to figure where they are, but the yacht must still be floating, and they're close."

The radio operator called the captain with the news. In moments the loudspeakers blared, "Emergency beeper on the *Marlin* still sending. We should be able to spot the boat!" The news increased everyone's hope.

The sky was darkening quickly. Soon the rain would begin. Worse, visibility would decrease greatly.

Just then, a cry went up from the bow and the upper watch at the same time. "Vessel, dead ahead!"

16

All eyes strained forward. Part of the yacht cabin and the bow could be seen. The entire stern of the boat was underwater. Two people clung to the cabin roof.

Because of the high waves, precautions were taken by the rescuers. The *Hawk* worked its way as close as possible, then lowered only one of its lifeboats. Since the lifeboat crew couldn't get too close without the danger of crashing, they expertly tossed life jackets to the men stranded on the yacht. Once the men had the life jackets on, the lifeboat threw a line to the men, and the boats were gently pulled closer together so the men could be helped on board.

Then, as if it had been waiting for the rescue, the yacht suddenly began to sink once again, and it slipped beneath the waves and disappeared before the lifeboat had returned to the *Hawk*. The men from the yacht were rushed to the ship's first-aid room for hot liquids and warm blankets.

The *Hawk* continued south to Keyport Harbor, former home port of the *Marlin*. The Ringers gathered with Ruth Ann and Lee in the mess hall. "I'm really proud of the way you kids are fitting in here on board," began Lee. "And Pete, I just can't tell you how important it was to everyone to know that the yacht was still floating. You and Jill didn't use your eyes, but you really used your heads."

"And speaking of heads," said Ruth Ann, laughing, "the people in the radio room are still shaking theirs. They can't get over you two! They don't want to let you go home when this cruise is over."

The Ringers, one and all, cheered and patted Pete and

Jill on the back. "Way to go, Peterola!" said Willy. "The gizmo guru strikes again."

"Congrats, Mr. and Mrs. Einstein," added Willy.

"Just don't let it go to your head," teased Jim.

Jill grinned widely and Pete sheepishly said, "Thank you, thank you." It seemed that whenever anyone accomplished something important, the whole gang shared the excitement.

"And just think," said Sam. "This is just the first day!"

THE END

For other adventures on this cruise, turn to page 32 and make different choices.

Or, turn to page 121.

18

Since they were now wide awake, Jill and Tina thought that seeing the storm was a great idea. Before they left their cabin, though, the girls each put on the rain gear they had been given. By the time they were ready, the ship had started to rock more violently.

"Now I know why people get seasick," said Jill.

When they came out on deck, the sounds of the nighttime storm were deafening. Except for the glare of the lights on deck, everything was dark, making the storm seem even more mysterious and powerful. Suddenly a shower of seawater drenched them both. Jill turned to Tina with water dripping off her face and shouted, "This is incredible!—See what I mean about the rain gear?"

Tina nodded in agreement. Then she noticed the beam of one of the searchlights directed toward the waves, and what she saw made her heart come up into her throat. She instinctively grabbed Jill with one hand, while she pointed with the other. "Look at those waves!" she exclaimed in awe. She found herself looking *up* at whitecaps. The *Eagle* was going up and down waves as if she was climbing mountains. Standing on deck, it was like the girls were on a wild roller coaster, and the wind in the rigging was howling like a thousand screaming kids.

At the bottom of the next wave, the *Eagle's* bow was buried for a terrifying instant in the sea, and a surge of water came sweeping along the deck. Before they could move, Tina and Jill lost their footing. Tina, the smaller of the two, felt herself being carried toward the edge of the deck. Frantically, she waved her arms trying to grab something. Her legs dropped over the side of the ship and the word *overboard* flashed in her mind like a huge neon sign, but at the last possible moment something closed tightly around her wrist and stopped her. The water passed her by and she looked up. She could hardly believe her eyes. Stretched out on the deck were Jill and a sailor. Jill was holding Tina by the wrist, and the sailor had hold of Jill by the ankle. His arm was hooked around the door entrance.

At first they lay there, stunned. Then the girls began to cry and laugh at the same time. The sailor pulled them to safety, and they hurried back inside, then gathered in a tight circle-hug for a long time. Finally, the sailor spoke. "Thank God you young ladies are safe. I'm glad I saw you when I did." Neither Tina nor Jill could think of anything to do except whisper thank-yous to the sailor—and to God.

They stood like that for a while, still recovering from the shock. Except for an occasional sniffle, no one moved or said anything.

Then Ruth Ann came by. "Oh, there you are! I found your bunks empty—" She stopped suddenly as she took in the situation. "Are you girls all right?"

"They're fine now," said the sailor, putting his hands gently on Tina's shoulders. "But kids, you'll be safer if you get back to your cabin and lie down. Here, let Ruth Ann help you get that rain gear off, and we'll get you into something warm and dry."

Tina cleared her throat and wiped her eyes. She moved slowly, almost like she was in a dream, as Ruth Ann helped her take off the rain gear. Meanwhile the sailor went to get her a heat-reflective blanket. Once back in her bunk, the exhausted Tina snuggled in her covers, where she shivered for a little while and then gradually relaxed and slipped back to sleep.

The next morning the girls found out, much to their amazement, that the boys had slept through the entire storm! When the girls told their story, the guys could hardly believe it. But Ruth Ann let them know it was all true.

As they were going back on deck after breakfast, Tina pointed out the sailor who had helped her. Jim slipped over to talk to him. "Thanks for . . . saving my sister," he said awkwardly, "I really . . . I guess I would have really missed her." Then he added in a whisper, "But don't tell her I said so!"

Tina, who was still nearby, said with a grin, "I heard *all* of that, big brother!"

CHOICE

Turn to page 78.

The five boys scooted down the railing to get a better look at the New York City skyline. Even the lights of Washington, D.C., which was across the river from Millersburg, seemed small in comparison to the millions of tiny "stars" of the New York City skyscrapers. The lights made interesting patterns on the dark shapes across the water. The Ringers were amazed. Lee approached and said, "Sometimes I stand here and watch those lights, too . . . all the people they represent. So many of them who live without ever knowing God. After my time in the service I think I'll stay in New York and try to help."

"Well, maybe some of us will be old enough to help too," said Willy.

"Well, I wasn't trying to recruit you for that job, yet," chuckled Lee, "but I sure appreciate a willing heart, Willy. OK guys, I think it's time to show you your quarters." He led them into the ship to a room he called "guest quarters." It was a tiny space with two sets of bunk beds, each stacked three beds high. Under the bottom bed were three slots just big enough to slide in a duffel. Their quarters were so small that they could hardly all stand in the room together. Some had to be on beds.

"Join the Coast Guard, become a sardine!" said Sam.

"I'll have to remember that for our next poster," said Lee, needling him. "But seriously, guys, I think it would be a good idea to call it a night. We'll be having a big day tomorrow, and it'll start early. When you come to breakfast, make sure you put on the life vest you find on your bunk. You'll be wearing those every day." He showed them where the "head" (bathroom) was and then said good night.

Willy lay back on his bunk and closed his eyes to remember all that had happened in the past couple of weeks since he had met Lee. He didn't notice when he stopped thinking and began dreaming.

The next thing he knew, Lee was shaking him and saying, "Time to get up, junior cadets! Let's get to breakfast. Then the captain will be telling us our mission for today."

It took the boys a while to figure out how to take turns dragging out their duffels, getting clothes, and then dressing. The first morning was complete chaos. They ended up using the spare bed to store their clothes. Lee stood in the doorway and chuckled.

On the way to breakfast, they ran into Ruth Ann, Jill, and Tina, who acted like they'd just been to a slumber party. It turned out they had the same size room for two of them that the boys had to share five ways. They began to kid each other, but the smells from the mess room reminded them how hungry they all were, and they attacked the eggs and bacon like starving sailors.

While they were eating, in walked the captain. All the sailors stood up immediately. Captain Miller was introduced to each of the kids, and he wished them a good time on their mission.

"Mission, sir?" said Willy in his most respectful tone.

"Yes, ladies and gentlemen, the United States Coast Guard has a mission for you!"

CHOICE

If the captain gets the gang involved in a training exercise, turn to page 61.

If they just observe, turn to page 75.

24

In a flash, Chris knew he had to tell someone. *After all,* he thought, *there's a chance I really did see someone, and that someone will need help.* "Lee," he shouted, "you're not going to believe this, but I'm almost positive I saw someone fall in the water from one of those sailboats!"

Lee immediately shouted some instructions, and several sailors with binoculars ran up to where he was standing. "Tell them where you saw the overboard, Chris," said Lee.

"Just as those three sailboats there were coming around that buoy," Chris said, pointing, "I saw someone fall out of the boat."

"There's one in the water!" shouted a sailor almost before Chris was finished. There were other orders given, and the *Hawk* turned toward the buoy. Other orders blared from the loudspeakers:

"All hands on deck!"

"Ready the lifeboats!"

"Rescue team ready!"

As the ship got nearer, the captain called to the person in the water, "Ahoy swimmer, can you signal?" There was no response. The person was being kept afloat by a life jacket, but there was no movement. In fact, sometimes the body was turned over and the person's face was in the water.

Everyone on the *Hawk,* including the Ringers,
realized this was a matter of life and death. Before the
cutter had stopped, the two lifeboats were already
swinging down. In each boat there were sailors dressed in
wet suits, prepared to go in the water. The outboard
motors were already running. As soon as the lowering
cables were free, the boats sprang away from the *Hawk.*

The Ringers were amazed by the teamwork of the
two lifeboats. The one in front passed right by the victim,
and two wet-suited sailors dropped into the water. The
next boat came slower and drifted carefully into position.
From there they helped lift the injured person onto a
stretcher and into their boat. They immediately backed
away and headed carefully back to the *Hawk,* while the
other lifeboat circled around and picked up their two
wet-suited sailors. A cheer went up from the Ringers.

In the meantime, the accommodation ladder had
been lowered so that the stretcher could be lifted up on
deck. By the time the victim arrived, the paramedic in the
lifeboat had already put on a neck brace and was checking
for injuries. As the stretcher was being lifted up onto the
deck, the kids saw that the person on it was a girl their
own age. She had a nasty purple bruise on her forehead,
but her eyes were open. She also looked a little confused.

"She got a bad bump on her head when she went
overboard, and that must have knocked her out for a
while. Except for that tender bruise, I think she'll be all
right," said the paramedic. The Ringers gathered around,
slapping Chris on the back and telling him, "Way to go!"

Meanwhile, the other lifeboat had caught up with the

26

racing sailboats and flagged them down. They were headed back to the *Hawk* now with two very concerned-looking parents. They rushed up the gangway and cried with relief when they saw their daughter was alive. The father explained, "Shelly doesn't usually sail with us when we're racing. We didn't even notice she was suddenly gone on the turn. I'm so sorry, honey."

He turned to Captain Miller with tears in his eyes. "I'm so grateful your men rescued my daughter," he began.

The captain smiled and said, "Glad to do it—it's our job. But you really need to thank this young man right here," he said, pointing at Chris. "He saw someone go overboard and let us know. Looks like having young people on board has already paid off!"

"Well, young man, those are sharp eyes you've got. Thank you for watching out for my daughter," said the dad, putting out his hand.

Chris wasn't used to having adults shake his hand, but this time it felt great. "Glad I could do it, sir," he said awkwardly.

"I'd like to say thanks, too, Daddy," said Shelly from the stretcher. The Ringers crowded around her again and introduced themselves. Their attention helped as much as the medical attention she had gotten. After a while, the lifeboat took her and her parents back to shore, where they promised they would have her checked out by a doctor, "Just to be sure."

That night at supper, Chris was surprised with a special presentation. The captain called for everyone's attention and said, "It is our custom on the *Hawk* to honor those who have given lifesaving service. Chris Martin, on behalf of the entire crew of the *Hawk,* we could not think of a better way to honor you than to make you and your Ringer friends honorary members of our crew." With that, he pulled out T-shirts for each of the kids. Each shirt had *"Hawk"* on the front stenciled in the shape of the cutter, and on the back each kid had his or her name and the title: "Crew member of the Coast Guard cutter *Hawk."*

Later, when Chris was going to sleep, he whispered a prayer of thanks to God for two good eyes. "Let me always use them to see ways to help others," he whispered as he drifted off to adventurous dreams.

THE END

Turn to page 121.

28

Willy said that he might not have time to help with the play, and that got Chris thinking. Finally, Chris said, "Look, Willy, if you go home now, I'm coming with you. I said I was gonna help you, and I really want to. And besides, I wanna hear more about that ship." He looked at Willy and smiled at the thought of their little drama back at the apartment. "And if you want to go and practice with Pastor Whitehead for a little while, I'll call Mom and ask if I can stay long enough to help you finish your work this evening."

Willy thought for a moment, then said, "I'll call home. If you can stay for supper, we can probably get it done."

The calls were made, and things worked out just right. Willy could be part of the play. Willy's mom especially appreciated his checking in. "From all the footprints outside, it looked like you had been carried off by a band of Bigfoots," she said.

"No, Mom," laughed Willy in return. "Those were just Chris and his big feet!"

Turn to page 88.

Charley hesitated, then turned and ran away. He was gone before anyone could even get to the gangway.

Pastor Whitehead sighed.

"What do you think, Grandpa?"

"I guess we'll just have to tell Jim. We'll wait till morning, though. No sense in waking him now. It's the first decent night of sleep he's had in a while." Pastor Whitehead and his grandson went back to keeping watch. They noticed nothing else unusual that night.

In the morning, they told Jim Wright about what had happened. He said nothing, just shaking his head and sighing.

Two days later, the *Niña II* was ready to set sail. The crew had arrived early and were rigging her sails and the other equipment she would need for her shakedown cruise. The Ringers were complimented several times on the thorough way in which they had cleaned up the ship. They called her "shining from stem to stern, from mast to keel." There had been no further problems with vandalism after the kids and Pastor Whitehead had come aboard.

About mid-morning the exciting moment arrived. The *Niña II* cast off lines and headed out to the Potomac channel for her maiden voyage. Unlike her namesake, the *Niña II* did have a small engine she could use when she was in a tight spot or if the wind didn't cooperate. It also helped for docking. As soon as she was out in the river, though, Mr. Wright ordered the sails set, and they began moving under wind power.

"It's so quiet," said Tina, standing with Jill up in the bow. "Just the soft sighs of the wind in the sails. I can see how someone would really come to love sailing." The small crew were busy with their tasks, and the other Ringers were scattered along the railing watching the shore of the Potomac glide past.

"Are we moving, or is the shore moving?" asked Jim.

"Actually," said Sam in his serious-professor tone of voice, "it's all done with mirrors, Jim," which earned him a friendly poke in the ribs.

Jill and Tina turned around and looked up at the sails. The large mainsail was clearly stenciled with the ship's name, *Niña II*. Tina began to daydream about what she would name a boat if she ever owned one. Suddenly, she felt Jill grip her arm like a vise. She looked at Jill and found her friend staring back at the stern of the ship and pointing with her free hand. Tina followed her eyes and saw, to her horror, smoke drifting out behind *Niña II*. Mr. Wright was in the cabin, steering, but he noticed the girls' actions up in the bow. He swung around and looked out the window. His mouth dropped open, and then he shouted, "Fire!"

The crew dropped what they were doing and came from different parts of the ship, each one carrying a fire extinguisher. They pulled the cover off the main cargo hold, and dark smoke belched out. The kids could hear Mr. Wright calling for help on the radio while the crew tried to battle the fire. Two of the crewmen rigged a hose and began to spray water into the hold. That put out the fire almost immediately.

One crewman took an extinguisher down into the hold to check for damage. He was back in a moment. "Someone rigged the engine to catch fire. If we hadn't caught her in time, the fuel tanks might have blown up and sunk us. That engine won't run again for a while."

Soon the *Niña II* was approached by a Coast Guard cutter that took her in tow. After hearing the situation, the Coast Guard captain said, "A diesel-engine fire was one of the few problems Columbus *didn't* have on his trip!" Then he added, "Hope you can get this repaired in a hurry, Mr. Wright. You've got a fine-looking vessel there. Wouldn't mind sailing on her myself sometime. . . ."

The Ringers agreed that even though their shakedown cruise had been the shortest in history, it had been exciting and worthwhile. Mr. Wright said, "The only shakedowns I know about that have been shorter than ours were sailed by ships that sank as soon as they were launched." He smiled, then added to Jill and Tina, "And I'm very thankful you girls saw the smoke when you did. Otherwise, we might all be part of the mess on the bottom of the Potomac River."

Jill and Tina, who were standing side by side, gave each other a squeeze. They were thankful, too.

THE END

Why would anyone want to sabotage a ship like the *Niña II?* To find out, turn to page 106 and make different choices along the way.

Or, turn to page 121.

Like having to choose between cake and ice cream, it was not an easy decision. But after grilling Lee with questions, the Ringers decided to head to New York City.

Much to everyone's relief, the next week went quite fast. Everyone got busy finishing school assignments, packing, and wondering what it would be like to be on the ocean.

"I wonder if we'll get to catch any drug smugglers or help the police capture criminals who are trying to escape by boat," said Pete as they were waiting impatiently on the front steps of the church for Lee to pick them up. The rest of the gang—Chris, Willy, Tina, Jim, Jill, and Sam—looked at each other like they were trying to decide who should straighten Pete out. But before anyone said anything, a new-looking van drove up with the words *Coast Guard* painted on its side. In smaller letters below that, it said, "Land-based Craft." Out jumped Lee and a young woman the kids had not met. After greeting everyone, Lee introduced them all to Ruth Ann, another Coast Guard recruiter who would be traveling with them.

"If things work out on this trip," said Lee, "Ruth Ann and I are hoping to do this more often so that other students can experience what life at sea is all about."

"Sounds good to me!" said Willy as he led the charge to load up the van. Everyone had packed their stuff in duffel bags, as Lee had instructed them, so getting in the van was a little like having a friendly oversized pillow fight. Finally all the bodies and bags were inside—even if they weren't necessarily in the right place.

Once the doors were closed, Ruth Ann yelled over the ruckus, "Everybody comfortable?"

Back came a chorus of "NO!" from the back of the van.

She laughed and said, "Well, welcome to the Coast Guard! Your discomfort is our number one priority." They took a few more minutes to get everyone settled.

Before they left, Lee said, "I don't think I'll be able to do this out loud on many of the trips I lead, so I'm going to enjoy this." He asked them all to pray with him, and he asked God to keep them all safe in their travels and adventures during the next week.

The kids were full of questions, and the five-hour trip across Maryland and New Jersey went quickly. They stopped to eat somewhere near Newark, and then crossed a long bridge that brought them into New York City. It was early evening when they pulled up to a military pier. Some of the kids were asleep, but they quickly woke up when the van entered the gate, past several armed guards. They drove along the pier and stopped by a large ship, which Lee introduced as the Coast Guard cutter *Hawk*.

Ruth Ann and the gang trudged up the gangway, each carrying their duffels, as Lee drove off to park the van. When they were officially allowed on deck by the watch at the top of the gangway, Ruth Ann told the boys she would take the girls to their cabin and that they should wait right where they were until Lee came for them.

"Wait?" queried Sam once Ruth Ann was out of earshot. "Methinks 'twould not be problematic to look around in the immediate vicinity." He waited for a reply from the rest of the guys.

CHOICE ⇌➤

If the boys decide to explore on their own, turn to page 59.

If the boys sit tight until Lee arrives, turn to page 21.

Sorry, buddy," mumbled Chris as he crowded by Willy on his way to the door, "but you know how hard it is to turn down an offer for ice cream!"

The Freeze was one of the unofficial hangouts of the Ringers. The other was the old Capitol Community Church, which had some hidden passageways and a lot of neat things to explore. Jim's grandfather, Pastor Whitehead, was the minister of the church and practically a member of the Ringers himself. The Freeze and the church were on opposite sides of a park in the center of town in Millersburg. Betty Metz, who ran the Freeze, really liked the Ringers. They, in turn, really liked the ice cream creations she was always inventing.

Chris stepped outside with Jim and Jill. He could almost taste the vanilla/root beer slush he knew he would order.

But suddenly he thought that maybe he had accepted Jim and Jill's invitation too quickly. He had heard Jim tell Willy they were sorry he couldn't go, followed by Willy's disappointed "That's OK" as he closed the door. Maybe he should have stayed and helped Willy. Besides, he didn't get to hear much about the *Amistad,* and he still wondered about Willy's strange answer.

Chris stopped so suddenly that his companions almost ran into him.

"What's up?" asked Jim.

"Well, I'm not sure I should go," said Chris sheepishly. "I think Willy was counting on my help. Maybe I should go back."

Jim and Jill said nothing, waiting as Chris stared blankly, thinking.

Chris quickly decided that he *had* to go back. It was the only thing a best friend could do, and he prided himself on being one of the best friends Willy had. He quickly explained to Jim and Jill and turned to go back. "You go on without me," he said.

As Chris turned, he glimpsed Willy ducking behind the corner evergreen. *Ah ha! Trying to sneak up on us, eh?* Chris thought to himself. He ran quickly toward the opposite side of the building so Willy wouldn't see him, made a huge snowball, then headed for the back, following his opponent's footprints to set up the perfect ambush. He went straight for the evergreen.

Neither boy saw the other coming through the thick branches, and the two collided head-on, snowballs exploding in their hands and sending spray in all directions. They were stopped in their tracks and fell over like they were in slow motion. Willy said, "Hey, Chris, we've got to stop meeting like this!"

After a moment, they got up and brushed themselves off again. "So what made you come back?" asked Willy.

Chris shrugged, trying not to seem too uncool. "I got hooked on this ship of yours. Why'd you come back out?"

Willy smiled with the same sort of sheepish smile Chris had given Jim and Jill. "I guess I changed my mind about passing up a trip to the Freeze." They laughed at each other.

"Well, Captain Washington, if you want to work on this history project of yours, I'm your slave. It's your call."

CHOICE ⇒

If Willy decides to go to the Freeze, turn to page 50.

If he finishes the ship, turn to page 62.

Jim let out a gasp and his heart stopped.

"Surprise!" said Marley. The sailor held Jim right where he was with the rope.

Jim smiled and let out a sigh of relief.

Then, very slowly, Marley let the rope out, lowering Jim about twenty feet right into the raft.

Jim was whooping and hollering all the way down. "It's great!" he shouted up to Willy. "Come on down!"

In a moment, Willy was standing where Jim had been a few minutes ago. Jim added his encouragement to Marley's instructions, and Willy was soon on his way down. As he was being lowered, there was another big gust of wind. Jim couldn't feel it on the side of the *Hawk* where the raft was, but a movement to his left caught his eye. On the side of another ship next to them, a sailor had been working from a scaffold, repainting the name of the ship on the stern. The gust of wind caught him off balance, and Jim noticed his flailing arms as he fell off the scaffold and into the bay.

Quickly, Jim pulled out the paddles from their sleeves. Just about then, Willy touched down in the raft. Jim shouted up to Marley, "Somebody just fell off the back of that ship. He's in the water."

Before Marley could say anything, Jim was paddling furiously. Willy grabbed the other paddle and began working on the other side. They covered the water between the ships quickly. Someone on the deck of the other ship was yelling at them to hurry.

At first, Jim and Willy could see no one. But those above them were shouting directions. When they got close, a sailor's arms and head broke the water for a moment. The raft was just close enough that Jim was able to grab a wrist and hold on. He heard a huge splash behind them. In a moment, Marley came swimming next to the raft and lifted the injured sailor out of the water. He was screaming in pain, saying he thought his back was broken.

Marley called up to the *Hawk* that a paramedic team was needed. "We can't lift this man into the raft without hurting him more. We'll need a backboard before we can take him out of the water."

Jim looked up and had an idea. He said, "Hey, what about lowering the scaffold all the way to the water? Then we can lay this guy on it like a stretcher!"

Marley looked up at the scaffold and then shouted, "Brilliant idea, squirt!" He quickly gave instructions to the sailors on deck to lower the scaffold all the way into the water. Using the raft for extra support, Marley was able to float the injured man right onto the boards. His shipmates gently lifted him back up, where the medical team from the *Hawk* was already waiting. Within minutes, an ambulance was on the scene and the sailor was taken to the hospital.

Meanwhile, others of the *Hawk's* crew had welcomed Marley, Jim, and Willy back on deck. When the cheering was over, Marley shook Jim's hand and said, "That was fast work and fast thinking, young man. That sailor may owe it to you if he walks again." Then he added, "Ya know, you squirts are a lot of fun to have around!"

"Yeah," answered Willy, "and just think how much fun it will be when we're actually trained to do this stuff!"

"Well, you may *all* have a shot at being sailors and heroes before this trip is over!"

THE END

This was only one of the many adventures the Ringers had on this trip. If you haven't found out about the slaver yet, or if you want to go aboard a tall ship, turn back to the beginning and make different choices along the way.

Or, turn to page 121.

Sam picked the wrong thing to joke about. "What is 'swabbing'? Is that where you clean the ship's ears?"

Two of the cadets winked at each other, and one of them quickly said, "You haven't been introduced to the pleasures of swabbing? Well, please allow us to show you." The rest of the kids looked questioningly at Ruth Ann and Lee, who just grinned.

Before any of the Ringers could ask "Is this really a good idea?" they all found themselves holding mops and buckets, standing on deck in their bare feet with their pants rolled up.

Meanwhile, one cadet explained that swabbing the decks was a time-honored and necessary tradition on sailing ships. "These decks get our tender loving care almost every day," he said. Then he suddenly yelled, "Let 'em go, boys!" Behind the kids, several cadets who had been standing with full buckets dumped them on the deck in the direction of the Ringers, so that icy water sloshed over their feet.

"Whooo! If I wasn't awake before, I sure am now," yelled Jim.

Once they were wet, there was no holding the Ringers back. They attacked the task of swabbing with gusto, much to the amusement of the sailors. The sailors also demonstrated their trick of standing shoulder to shoulder while they swabbed, so that a wide section of the deck could be worked on. In no time at all there was a race on—Ringers along the port side, sailors along the starboard. Suds were flying, swabbers were slipping, and there was more laughing than mopping getting done.

"Boy, is this ever fun!" yelled Sam between gasps and grunts.

One of the sailors yelled back, "Not when you have to do it every day, kid!"

He was right, but everyone just laughed.

CHOICE

Turn to page 55.

Let's wait and see if we hear anything else," whispered Chris. "If there's anybody snooping around, they're bound to make more noise."

The others nodded in silent agreement, and without any further discussion, the three got comfortable again and halfheartedly resumed their watch. They heard nothing else, and Jim and his grandfather relieved them at 3:00 A.M..

Jim and his grandfather were on their second stroll along the deck when they saw someone moving cautiously along the dock. At that moment, they were at the other end of the ship from the cabin. There was no chance to warn the others. They crouched down and waited.

Soon a single dark figure climbed up the gangway and moved across the deck. Pastor Whitehead stood up suddenly and shined his flashlight into a pair of startled eyes. "Charley Wright, what are you doing here?"

"Who—who are you?" the boy answered in a scared voice.

"I'm Leonard Whitehead, your dad's friend. He told me you haven't been getting along lately. Have you been vandalizing your dad's project?"

44

CHOICE ⇔

What will Charley do? If he runs away, turn to page 29.

If Charley answers Mr. Whitehead, turn to page 82.

The next day when the kids gathered at church to ring the bell, they found a sharp-looking young man waiting for them in his Coast Guard uniform. Everyone was introduced to Lee, including Pastor Whitehead, who had also arrived early to let the Ringers in. Lee got a real kick out of watching them take turns waking up the town on Sunday morning.

"This reminds me of living on a ship!" he shouted over the ringing of the bell.

When the ringing in everyone's ears had faded a little, Sam asked Lee, "How does this remind you of living on a ship?"

Lee told the kids about how bells are used on ships to refer to the different times of the day. Each day is broken into six watches of four hours each, and the beginning of each watch is marked by a single bell. Then another ring is added every half hour. "So when you hear eight bells, your watch is over," explained Lee.

"Well, having a bell go off every half hour would sure keep me awake!" declared Sam.

The gang didn't see Lee during their Sunday class with Mrs. Whitehead because Pastor Whitehead was talking to him. Lee sat right in the front row during church, and when the Ringers acted out the shipwreck of Paul the apostle, he really laughed. (They did the motions while

Pastor Whitehead read the story.) Pastor Whitehead used the Ringers' Scripture skit to help make the point that even when things seem completely out of control, God is still in control. He explained during his sermon that his conversation with Lee about sailing had helped him put the final touches on his message. He also announced that there would be a brief meeting of all the Ringer parents right after the morning worship service. There was a soft chuckle from the congregation. Everyone knew what the pastor meant.

In the meeting with the parents, Lee explained that he had managed to arrange for two possible adventures for the gang during spring break from school. The kids began elbowing each other like crazy! Each possibility would involve being away for several days. Lee could take them to New York City to experience life on one of the cutters that patrols the coast. Or, they could go to New London, Connecticut, and be involved in a shakedown cruise of a tall ship called the *Eagle*.

After asking some questions, the parents left it up to the Ringers to decide.

CHOICE ➯

If the Ringers decide to ride the cutter as it patrols the New York coast, turn to page 32.

If they decide to go to New London for the shakedown of the *Eagle*, turn to page 4.

Once the three decided to investigate, Sam volunteered. "Only one of us should go, 'cause that will make less noise," he whispered. "You guys stay here—no, wait. Go tell the others." He slowly got to his feet and quietly walked past the hold opening. The clouds gave way to the moon as Sam snuck past, and he felt like a sitting duck. But the extra light helped him see where to put his feet, so he chose his steps carefully.

Unfortunately, he was being so careful about where to step that he wasn't watching where the rest of him was going. He bumped into an unlit lantern that was hanging above the deck, and before he could do anything, there was a flash of glass in the moonlight and a terrible crash as the lantern hit the deck and shattered.

Sam shrieked, then froze. Almost at the same moment, a thud came from down in the hold.

Sam shouted, "All right guys, let's get 'em!" He began running furiously in place on the deck. Almost instantly, Chris and Tina joined him in the noisemaking. But they all stopped abruptly when they were interrupted by loud cries of pain below in the hold. The cries were mixed with noises from the cabin as everyone else on board tried to make sense of what was going on. When they all arrived, Sam warned them not to step on the glass and told them that the cries were coming from some unknown person in the hold.

Pastor Whitehead had brought along several powerful flashlights. He climbed up on the housing that held the hold cover and flashed his light inside. No one could miss the sounds of anguish below. Pastor Whitehead sent Jill and Chris to call the police and an ambulance from the pay phone on the dock. Then Sam and Jim climbed down the ladder while the others shone lights for them to see. Their lights fell on a boy, clutching his leg in pain.

"Is your leg broken?" asked Sam.

The boy nervously nodded yes, and he cried out and began to shake uncontrollably.

Sam began to take off his coat, and the boy shook his head frantically. "We're not going to hurt you." Sam held out his coat. "You need to stay warm."

Sam and Jim kneeled beside him and waited with him as he bit his lip. Almost automatically, Jim prayed. " . . . and Father, please help—" Jim stopped.

"Charley," the boy said.

"Please help Charley. Comfort him, and just make the pain go away. And please let his leg be all right."

The paramedics arrived and confirmed that the boy's leg was broken. He had fallen when Sam bumped into the lantern. Mr. Wright came close as the paramedics worked. "Charley, you were doing all this stuff? Why?"

"I didn't think you were telling the truth when you said you were going to have to lay us off because you were out of money. I guess I wanted to teach you a lesson. I was going to plant an igniter next to the engine so the ship would blow up the first time you put her to sea," the boy confessed. "I didn't count on getting ambushed." He turned to Sam. "Thanks for helping me."

"That's OK," said Sam. "Hate to see anybody hurt."

"Charley," said Pastor Whitehead, "Sam just treated you the way Jesus wants to treat you if you give him a chance. I'd like to talk to you about it sometime."

"Well, I'll probably be in jail, so I won't be hard to find," said Charley sadly.

Mr. Wright patted his shoulder and said, "We'll see about that, Charley. We'll see about that."

Mr. Wright was able to sail the *Niña II* during spring break after all. But with all that had gone on, he decided to play it safe and not sail with guests on board until he was absolutely sure she was safe. In the meantime, he also arranged for Charley not to go to jail, but to work off his sentence by working on the *Niña II* once his leg healed. As Mr. Wright said, "After all, it was the least I could do for my own son."

Pastor Whitehead later told the Ringers that Jim Wright and his son had been having difficulties for a long time, but that now things finally seemed to be getting better. "Both of them needed to give God a little more room to work in their hearts," said Pastor Whitehead with a smile.

THE END

Turn to page 121.

I call it rocky road," said Willy. "Let's head for da Freeze."

"A man of true nobility," said Chris dramatically, placing his hand on Willy's shoulder, "passes up having a slave." The two friends brushed off the remaining snow as they followed in the footsteps recently laid by Jim and Jill, heading for their ice-cream hangout. Though it was snowy, the sun was bright and warm as they walked.

"Yeah," added Willy quietly. "That's more than you can say about the crew of the *Amistad.*"

"Hey, you never did finish explaining. Just what was the deal with that thing?"

"Well, it was a slaving ship."

"No way."

"*Yes* way."

Chris waited for Willy to go on. The seriousness of the topic quickly changed the atmosphere of the post-snowball-fight silliness. "Well, what happened?" Chris finally said.

Willy got a faraway look in his eyes. Chris thought his friend to be a good storyteller, and he wondered what he would learn about the *Amistad*.

"Ships called *slavers* brought captured African men, women, and children across the ocean to be slaves here," began Willy. "Many of the people died on the way, because they were packed inside the ships like baggage.

And there wasn't enough food, so people got sick. It must have been gross! I wonder sometimes what happened to my relatives when they came across." Willy stopped for a moment, as if he was on some kind of mental journey. Chris couldn't think of anything to say, so he just waited. Willy went on. "One of the most famous slaving ships was the *Amistad*. She didn't pick up slaves in Africa, though. She was used to move slaves from Cuba into the States."

"How long ago did this happen?" asked Chris.

"The trip that made the *Amistad* famous happened about a hundred and fifty years ago, in 1839," answered Willy.

Chris tried to remember some other dates to fit with the one Willy had just mentioned. "So this happened before Lincoln freed the slaves," he said.

"Yes," answered Willy, "but a lot of people don't know that bringing slaves from Africa was supposed to stop long before the slaves were freed. There were Navy ships along the coast here and near Africa trying to stop the slave trade. But some slaves were still being shipped over here. The *Amistad* was one of the ships used to smuggle slaves into the U.S."

"So what happened to the ship?"

"Well, before they got to the States, the slaves rebelled and took over the ship—"

"Hey, I never heard of any slaves taking back a ship before!" Chris exclaimed. "How did they get away? Weren't they kept in chains and stuff?"

"Yes they were," answered Willy. "But every once in a while, the slaves had to be brought out on deck to exercise a little and breathe some fresh air. The people in charge weren't being nice, they just wanted to protect their investment and make sure the slaves arrived healthy enough to sell."

Chris shook his head in disbelief. "How could people treat other people that way?" he thought out loud.

"You're asking me?"

"Gross."

"One day they had some weather problems, and the crew couldn't sail in the direction they wanted to go. Then, because the trip was taking longer, they began to run out of water. The slaves had to suffer even more than usual."

"How many slaves were there?" asked Chris, trying to imagine himself chained in the dark hold of a ship.

"There were forty-nine slaves and seven sailors on board. But it wasn't how many slaves there were that mattered—one of them happened to find a nail during his exercise time."

"That's not much of a weapon to go against guns!" exclaimed Chris.

Willy chuckled and said, "It is when you use it to pick locks. The leader among the slaves was a chief's son named Cinque. He managed to hide the key in his armpit when they were taken back into the hold and locked up. At night, when the crew were sleeping from fighting the storm, the slaves broke free and took over the ship. Some of the crew were killed and some jumped overboard. By morning, only three of the crew were left on the ship. Cinque saved their lives because he knew the slaves would need help to sail."

"I hadn't thought of that," said Chris. "The slaves

probably wouldn't know how to sail. Then what happened?"

"The slaves wanted to go back to Africa, so they forced the crew to sail east," continued Willy. "But the crew tried to trick the slaves. During the day, when the sun showed everyone what direction they were sailing in, the crew sailed east, but at night, they sailed north, toward the States."

"Oh, man, I hope they got away," wished Chris out loud.

"In a way, they did," said Willy, much to Chris's relief. "The *Amistad* began to see other boats as she sailed along the coast of the U.S., but they got as far as Long Island, New York, before a Navy ship captured them."

"Did Cinque and the others have to become slaves? I thought you said they got away!" asked Chris in rapid fire.

"Well, the slaves were taken to court, but they were eventually freed. Their story was told all over the States. The almost-slaves became famous, and some of them, including Cinque, did get back to Africa. Different church groups in the States helped them try to get home and find their families. I guess, though, that most of their families had been taken as slaves. So going home was pretty sad."

Chris thought about the tiny model ship again. "I know your people didn't have a choice about coming to America," he said softly. "But I'm glad it worked out for you and me to be friends."

Willy nodded. "Amen, brother. Thank God for that." He paused, and then continued. "I decided to build the ship because it helped me understand some things about

54

American history," said Willy. "Makes me mad that they used a ship called 'Friendship' to carry slaves, but since you and I worked on it together, I'll think of it as our 'friend-ship,'" he said, then added, "Friend . . . *ship*. Get it?"

"Yeah, I get it, you landlubber!" Chris mock-shouted at his buddy.

"Ahoy, Matey, ice cream ho!" yelled Willy, pointing to the Freeze as it came into view. Salt and Pepper, as they were known at school, broke into a final sprint to their destination, bumping each other along the way.

THE END

Turn to page 121.

After their first day at sea, the Ringers were exhausted. That night the weary gang met with Lee and Ruth Ann out on deck beneath the stars.

Lee read John 3:1-21 from the Bible. They were all familiar with the story of Nicodemus, the man who came to Jesus at night to talk. Jesus told him he had to be born again, and Nicodemus, who was pretty educated, couldn't figure out what Jesus meant. Jesus explained that people can be born a second time by beginning a personal relationship with God.

Ruth Ann reread verse 8, which says, "Just as you can hear the wind but can't tell where it comes from or where it will go next, so it is with the Spirit. We do not know on whom he will next bestow this life from heaven." Then Ruth asked, "In what ways is the Holy Spirit like wind?"

"Well, we can sure hear the wind up in the sails and the rigging," said Willy.

"And there's no doubt it's powerful," said Jim.

"You're not kidding," said Willy. "It moves this ship like it was a little toy."

"And if the sailors don't cooperate with the wind, they won't get where they want to go," offered Jill.

Tina quietly added, "Dad always says you can't tell whether God's Spirit is really in a person when they're stopped, but as they move through life, you'll be able to see from the way they live whether or not they are being moved by his Spirit."

"Yeah, yeah!" said Chris, excited about his discovery, "so one of the things we have to do is expect the Spirit to work in us like the way sailors lift a ship's sails expecting the wind to blow. Not paying attention to the Spirit is like a ship that never sets its sails!"

"Exactly," concluded Lee, "when we live by God's Spirit, we don't always know where he's going to blow us. We just need to obey when he shows us the way."

There were several yawns as the kids thought about their discussion. Ruth Ann offered a brief prayer and they all went off to bed, anticipating more excitement the next day.

Suddenly Tina found herself on the floor. It was the middle of the night, and she had fallen out of her bunk. She wasn't hurt, just confused. She struggled to her feet, only to discover that the cabin floor was so slanted she couldn't stand straight.

Jill's groggy voice came out of the darkness. "What's happening?" she mumbled, turning on her flashlight. She had been awakened when she had rolled up against the wall on her side of the tiny cabin they shared with Ruth Ann.

"I don't know," answered Tina as she clung to the post of her bunk. She wished Ruth Ann was there to tell tham everything was OK. The floor of the cabin came back to normal, then tipped again. "I think we're in a storm."

Jill came wide awake with interest. "Hey! Let's go ouside and take a look."

"I don't think that's a good idea," cautioned Tina.

The cabin tilted again.

"No, c'mon! It'll be cool! This is our chance to see a real storm at sea!—'AND YOU . . . ARE . . . THERE!'" Jill said dramatically.

"But isn't it dangerous?"

"Well, you're the one who fell out of bed!" said Jill. "Here. Let's get our rain gear on. Then we should be O.K."

The cabin continued to rock.

CHOICE ⇒

Seeing a storm at sea could be awesome! On the other hand, it could be dangerous, too. If Jill and Tina stay put, turn to page 101

If they decide to go out and see the storm, turn to page 18.

58

Indeed, the Ringers are studious and eager to learn. But during spring break, the adventurous, never-say-die Ringers seize the day. They don't just visit anywhere—they explore; they wander; they have *adventures!*

CHOICE

So turn to page 84.

Yeah, guys," said Chris in his take-charge tone, "here's a chance to explore on our own. Let's move out!"

"Hold it. I don't think that's a good idea," said Pete in his usual cautious tone.

"Come on," chimed in Willy, "we're already past the guards. Who can stop us now?"

"I think I can!" said a deep, powerful voice from the shadows behind them. Out from the dark stepped what they all agreed later was the biggest human being any of them had ever seen.

All five boys jumped. "I believe you!" said Willy.

The sailor's face split into a beautiful grin as he said, "You must be the squirts Lee told us he was bringing on board. Two minutes on my deck and you're already trying to get in trouble. But I'm going to do my best to keep you out of it! I'm Seaman Marley—but you can call me 'sir,'" he said with a deep laugh.

Chris thought to himself, *I can't think of anything other than "sir" that I would call him anyway!*

"Now listen, I've got other things to do. You squirts think you can keep from falling overboard until Lee gets here?" asked Marley.

There weren't any arguments.

"Good. Now stay out of trouble and don't go anywhere." He walked away, chuckling at the kids' reaction.

60

CHOICE

Turn to page 21.

The Ringers all looked at each other, unsure of what he meant.

"What we would like to do," explained the captain, "is give you kids some basic water-survival training and also have you help us by letting my men practice rescuing you. We do a lot of patrolling work in the Coast Guard, but the biggest share of our duty is finding and rescuing people. Sometimes they've been washed overboard, sometimes they've lost their boat, or maybe they just plain got lost. Are you kids game to try?"

"Sounds like fun!" said Willy, while the others nodded. Everyone, that is, except Sam.

Tina, who was sitting next to him, noticed and said, "You're suddenly quiet, Sam. What's wrong?"

Sam had never learned how to swim. Somehow, the idea of having to go *in* the water had not occurred to him in all the excitement about this trip. He was a little ashamed to have to admit to his friends now that he was afraid of the water.

But he was on the spot. He had to say something.

CHOICE ⇒

If Sam confesses, turn to page 12.

Will Sam cover up the fact that he can't swim? If so, turn to page 110.

My *slave,* huh?" Willy said thoughtfully, rubbing his chin for effect. "I like, I like."

The two friends went inside, took off their coats, then huddled around the pieces of Willy's emerging model of the *Amistad.*

"OK, I've got an important job for you while I'm cutting out these sails," said Willy. He handed Chris the longest tweezers Chris had ever seen. Then he pointed out two small U-shaped pieces of wood that were connected by a square piece of wood about the size of a large matchstick. He picked up the ship hull and placed it into the U-shaped pieces. Chris could see that the fit was perfect. "Use the tweezers and that special glue to put this mount for the ship inside the bottle," instructed Willy. He showed Chris how to do it and where to glue the mount.

As Chris was sliding the mount into the bottle, he noticed again how small the opening was. "Are you sure you can get *that* boat in *this* bottle, Willy?" he asked.

"If not, I'm going to be *extre-ee-emely* upset!" answered Willy. "I'm following these directions exactly. This was one of the only kits I could find for a ship in a bottle." He looked at Chris. "Most people who make these actually carve out their models by hand. I would have done that too, but I lacked T.N.T."

"What did you lack?" asked Chris, knowing Willy had set him up for a punch line.

"Time 'n' talent—T.N.T.!" said Willy with an almost-straight face.

"Well, I don't know about time," said Chris, "but it looks to me like you'll still need a lot of talent to get that boat into the bottle."

"What I need for *that* starts with *T*—but it isn't talent," answered Willy. He picked up two pieces a little larger than toothpicks. "These are the masts. The *Amistad* had two of them. She was the kind of ship they called a schooner." At one end of each mast was a tiny wire which went through the wood and was bent down on both sides toward the end of the mast. Willy picked up the ship's hull and fitted each of the masts to the holes in the deck that lined up with the wires. "Now," he said, "take each of these back out and put a really small drop of glue on the ends of the wire, and stick them back into the deck. And make sure you don't get glue on the mast itself."

Chris did what he was told, but he noticed that the masts wouldn't stand up straight. The wires were like hinges and the masts fell right over. "You sure you don't want some glue on the masts to make them stand up?" asked Chris.

"If you do that," said Willy, "I'll be in big *T* for trouble. That's not the kind of *T* I need." He took a short stick and glued it so it stuck out from the front of the hull.

"What's that for?" asked Chris.

"It's called a *bowsprit,*" answered Willy, "but it also makes it possible to get this ship in the bottle."

Chris sat back and watched Willy carefully tie threads to the masts and the sides of the ship. All the lines were threaded through a small hole in the bowsprit. After the lines were in place, Willy carefully glued the sails on the masts. Little by little the small pieces began to look like a real ship. Chris couldn't keep himself from saying, "You know, if you were a married Navy captain, when your wife came home tonight you could say, 'Sorry, honey, I shrunk the ship!'"

"Very funny," said Willy, who was concentrating on glueing the last sail in place. He moved away from the ship and smiled a pleased smile. He turned to his friend and asked, "What do you think?"

"I think she looks great, but you're gonna bust her all up to get her in that bottle."

"Not if the big *T* works," said Willy with a big smile. He picked up the ship, and to Chris's amazement, gently pushed the mast at the back (stern) of the ship down. Because of the way in which the thread had been tied from one mast to the other to the bowsprit, both masts now laid down on top of the ship into a neat little narrow package. Chris suddenly realized why the masts were on hinges—they had to be in order for the ship to fit through the neck of the bottle.

"Wow!" he said. "That is so cool! That is so great! That is amazing! So that's how the big *T* works."

"Just the tricks o' me trade, mate," answered Willy in his best sailor talk. "No talent, mate, just *tricks!*"

Using a long bamboo skewer, Chris put some glue on the mount where the ship would rest. Then he held the bottle steady while Willy picked up the ship using the long tweezers. He ever-so-gently slid the collapsed ship into the bottle and set her hull into the mount.

"I see it, but I hardly believe it," muttered Chris under his breath.

"OK," sighed Willy, "just one more tricky part." Still holding the boat with the tweezers, he began to cautiously pull on the long threads that ran into the bottle, through the bowsprit, and onto the masts and rigging. As if by magic, the masts slowly stood up and the sails hung just as if they were full of wind. Willy had been holding his breath, but he let it out with a long, low whistle. He gently released the threads, pulled the tweezers out of the bottle, turned to his friend and said, "ALL RIGHT!" at the top of his lungs.

Chris was so surprised he jumped.

"That's for getting me at the window a while ago," said Willy, laughing for joy.

Chris just shook his head and looked at the project. He didn't know what to say. Willy had done a great job. Finally, he cleared his throat and said, "Well, Mr. Washington, what you have here is a really fine boat—err ship—err schooner. Looks like about an *A* to me!"

"Well, if it ain't, I'll make someone walk the plank, mate," said Willy in a sailor roar.

Willy put another drop of glue right at the place where the lines ran through the bowsprit. After that was dry, he used his razor knife with a curved blade to carefully cut the threads that trailed out the bottle. The ship was done.

"That's it, huh?" asked Chris.

"That's it." The two sat there admiring their creation.

"Too bad we can't sail on a real ship," said Chris wistfully.

"We can."

"Yeah, right."

"I'm serious."

Chris stared at Willy to decide how much truth was in this declaration. "You're serious?"

Willy nodded.

"When?"

"Let's head over to the Freeze first and see if anybody's there."

"Don't make me wait. Tell me now."

"Come on, let's go." Willy got up.

"Let me get this straight," said Chris. "You're my best friend, right?"

"Right!" answered Willy.

"We've been through thick and thin together!" continued Chris.

"Right!" said Willy again.

"We're Ringers all the way!" said Chris.

Willy was beginning to laugh, but managed to compose himself and say, "Right!"

"And you're going to make *me* wait to hear this good news?"

Willy practically shouted. *"Right!"*

Before Chris could argue, Willy grabbed his coat and headed for the door. With Chris right behind him, he ran practically all the way to the Freeze, three blocks away. Spring break was well in hand.

THE END

If you don't know what Willy is talking about, turn to page 1 and make different choices along the way.

Chris shrugged his shoulders and sighed. "All right, all right," he repeated, imitating Willy. "I'm coming, I'm coming." The two went toward Willy's room. "What's so totally cool about your history project that you can't peel yourself away?" He tried to dry his hair by flicking it around with his hand.

"I'm gonna build a ship, with masts and sails and stuff—and I'm gonna do it *inside a bottle,*" answered Willy as he entered his room. He stopped to wad up his dripping socks. On Willy's desk was a large, clear, glass bottle.

"Is this where you're going to build your boat—in a bottle?" he asked, joking.

"That's the one," said Willy seriously. "Only it's a *ship,* not a boat, you landlubber!" He got some dry socks from the dresser and tossed his wet ones through the bathroom door, banking off the medicine cabinet mirror and into the sink. "Three points!"

"Landlubber?" said Chris in mock disgust. "You're the one who looks like you just fell overboard!" Chris picked up the bottle and looked inside. "You've got some room in here, but there's a little problem. Have you noticed?" he asked, pointing at the opening in the neck. "How are you going to work on the boat—uhhh, *ship*—through such a small hole?" Chris put the bottle up to his eye and looked down into it.

"Well," began Willy, "I—"

"Getting your head through here is really gonna hurt! Of course, once you get inside this thing, you better stay there. I'll help from outside and hand in whatever you need to build your ship. Hey, wait a minute. With you inside this bottle, where is the ship gonna fit?"

"That's a great idea!" said Willy with mild sarcasm. "I hadn't figured on getting *in* the bottle to build the ship."

"OK, really. How are you going to do it?" asked Chris, curious to find out Willy's plan. "You gotta have special tools to reach into the bottle and do the work. This is really gonna take a long time!"

Instead of answering, Willy went over to his closet and brought out a large piece of thick, stiff cardboard. On it, Chris could see the hull of a small ship and piles of tiny parts scattered around. Willy set everything down on the floor, and both boys bent over the project.

"Is this awesome-cool or what?" whispered Chris. "How long have you been working on this?"

"Man, it seems like forever," sighed Willy. "Even though it's supposed to be the fast way, it still takes a lot of time. And I even started with most of the pieces already cut for me!"

"So c'mon! What's the secret? How do we build the ship in the bottle?" asked Chris, growing impatient but becoming interested.

"That's just it, we don't build it *in* the bottle, buddy. We build it *outside* the bottle and then put it inside!" Willy was happy to be showing Chris something new.

"What? Really?" exclaimed Chris. "I don't see how."

"In that case, you'll have to wait and see." Willy just sat there and smiled.

"OK, you got me. What can I do to help?"

"You can help me make the stand I'll use to display the bottle," instructed Willy. He handed Chris a rough plank and some short pieces of dowel. They went back outside to the garage, and Willy showed Chris how to use the small drill press he had set up. They drilled four slanted holes the exact size of the dowels in the plank, and then Willy had Chris cut four dowel lengths, about three inches long. These they stuck with glue into the plank so that the dowels held the bottle on its side without rolling or wiggling.

Back in his room, Willy said, "The stand is perfect. Now all it lacks is the nameplate." He handed Chris a small, rough piece of wood on which was painted, in rough letters, the word *Amistad*. "Glue this onto the plank right . . . here," he took a pencil and marked the spot, "but make sure it's real straight."

In just a few minutes, Chris was done. "What does *'Amistad'* mean, Willy?"

"It's supposed to mean 'friendship,' but it really wasn't a very friendly ship," Willy said under his breath as he concentrated on the tiny sail he was cutting out of paper with a razor-blade knife.

Chris was puzzled by Willy's answer, as well as his friend's tone. "Why did you pick that name to call your bo—I mean ship?"

The conversation was interrupted by a knock at the door. Willy jumped to his feet. "Hold on. I gotta get the door."

Chris came out of Willy's room just in time to see Jim and Jill enter. Jill was Chris's cousin, and she had been spending the week with Chris's family since her school had a different spring vacation. Jim Whitehead was one of the original Ringers, along with Willy, Chris, Jill, and some others. The Ringers had a way of making things exciting around Millersburg without really trying.

"Oh, hi, Chris," said Jill, spotting Chris. "I wondered where you were. What are you guys up to?"

"We've been working on a school project," said Willy.

"You got time for a run down to the Freeze with us?" asked Jim.

Without thinking, Chris said, "Of course. We're outta here!" He turned to get his coat from Willy's room.

Willy just stood there. "I don't think I can go, guys. I'd really like to finish the project."

Now Chris wasn't sure what to do.

CHOICE ➡

If Chris leaves Willy to go with Jim and Jill to the Freeze, turn to page 35.

If Chris tries to talk Willy into coming with them, turn to page 8.

Even though he knew about the way this satellite stuff worked, Pete wasn't sure he could actually operate the receiver. So he and Jill returned to deck, where they discovered that in the few minutes they had been gone, the wind had increased and the waves had gotten bigger. Now the water was washing over the bow of the *Hawk* as she plowed ahead.

Over on the port-side rail, Sam and two sailors were yelling and pointing. The wind was so loud it was hard to hear. "—ber raft!" Others joined them, and a powerful searchlight swung in the direction they were pointing. On the crest of a wave, they saw the bottom of an overturned rubber raft. In bright yellow paint, almost hidden by the water, was the word *Marlin*, upside down.

The *Hawk* was quickly steered in that direction, and a long pole with a hook snagged the raft and brought it on board. There was no one in it, and no signs that it had been used at all. The cutter began to search in bigger and bigger circles around the place where they had found the raft, hoping to locate any survivors. The rest of the day was spent searching, but no trace of the yacht was found. At dark, the search was called off. By then, the weather had improved a little and another ship had joined the search.

The kids were upset, and they noticed the crew was

more quiet than when they had come on board. Later that evening, Sam asked Lee about it.

"Well, most of us really enjoy the challenge of finding and saving people who are stranded or in trouble at sea. And when we fail, we take it hard. We wonder if it was our fault," explained Lee.

Tina asked, "What do you think happened?"

"We'll probably never know," answered Ruth Ann. "They had enough time to send a distress signal and launch their raft. Maybe their boat just sank too quickly. Or maybe they had an accident trying to get into the raft. Or the raft may have capsized once they were in it. The seas were rough today. If they weren't wearing life vests, there was little hope of survival."

"One of the reasons for this trip," said Lee, "is to teach you some basic survival practices for water safety. Most people who die in these kinds of accidents don't have to. It's their lack of preparation that kills them."

"So what happens now?" asked Willy.

"Well, we'll stay in this area tonight, then search some more in the morning," Ruth Ann said, then paused. "You kids have seen some of the kind of work we do here in the Coast Guard. I hope you learn a lot while you're with us—" she sighed—"and I hope we don't have any more misses."

Jill had been very quiet during the conversation. Now she said softly, "I think it would be good for us to pray for the families of those who may have died here today." They all felt that was important, so they took turns praying. After that, they wandered off to bed.

In their bunks with the lights out, the boys were

unusually quiet. Finally, Jim said, "When you think about all the lives in danger out here at sea, you realize this work is really worth doing." Out of the darkness several voices murmured agreement.

They all went to sleep wondering what the next day would bring.

THE END

As the Ringers found out, failures and disappointments are just as much a part of life as the good times. If you want to see what else happened to them, or if you want to find out more about Coast Guard ships, turn to page 45 and make different choices along the way.

Or, turn to page 121.

We're going to patrol along the coast of New Jersey and Delaware for several days. I'd like you kids to observe our work, and if there's opportunity, participate in some of our exercises. We'll be casting off in an hour," explained the captain.

The Ringers just nodded and said, "Yes, sir!"

After they finished breakfast, they stood on deck and watched a flurry of activity as the sailors prepared to sail. Lee and Ruth Ann stayed with them, explaining many of the details of what was going on. "It looks like everyone is just rushing around, doesn't it?" asked Ruth Ann. "But each person on a ship like this has many specific duties to do. Everyone depends on everyone else to do their part."

"Is there something we can do?" asked Tina.

"I'm glad you asked that," said Lee. "Marley mentioned a job he could use all of your help doing." He led the gang to find Seaman Marley, the huge sailor some of them had met the night before.

Marley greeted them with a big smile and said, "So this is my new work crew! Well, I'll try to go easy on them. Follow me, ladies and gentlemen." He herded the Ringers toward the front of the ship until they came to two small wooden lifeboats sitting on deck. "Because our cutter is so large," Marley explained, "sometimes when we are involved in a rescue we have to launch these smaller boats to do the delicate work. But yesterday they were used for cleaning the harbor scum off the *Hawk,* and now we're going to clean them off!"

As if by magic, the kids found their hands full of brushes, buckets, and scrapers. "Heave to, mates!" said Marley as they scrubbed the grime and seaweed off the lifeboats. Then they hosed down the boats and, under Marley's direction, helped several sailors lift each of the boats into its spot so that it could easily be swung overboard for a rescue. Then Marley gave them their first lesson in swabbing the decks, and while they were working, he taught them a song. He would sing a line, and they would repeat it after him. It went:

It's time to swab the decks, (*It's time to swab the decks,*)

Because I've got a hunch, (*Because I've got a hunch,*)

If we don't get them squeaky clean, (*If we don't get them squeaky clean,*)

There won't be any lunch! (*There won't be any lunch!*)

As they were finishing the second boat, the call came over the loudspeaker on board, "Cast off!" The thick lines that connected the *Hawk* to the pier were pulled on board and coiled. The ship began to move slowly toward open water.

Just before the *Hawk* reached the end of the pier, Lee instructed the kids to look to their left as they entered the main harbor. There across the water, shining brightly in the early morning sun, was the Statue of Liberty. The Ringers let out a chorus of "oohs" and "aahs."

The harbor was full of boats and ships of many sizes. Lee pointed out some of the landmarks that were possible to see, such as the Empire State Building and the World Trade Center. The famous Staten Island Ferry was passing by ahead of them.

Chris's attention was drawn to a group of smaller sailboats that seemed to be racing. Three of the boats were approaching a bright buoy and were obviously going to make a turn around it. They were close enough so that he could make out individual people scrambling on each of the sailboats. Chris was fascinated by all the activity.

As the boats made the turn, they nearly collided. There was a moment of confusion as the sails were adjusted for the new direction, and Chris was sure he saw someone fall off the boat that made the widest turn. At least, he *thought* he saw a bright yellow life jacket tumble over the side of the boat. He rubbed his eyes to make sure, but he couldn't see anyone in the water. He expected the boat to stop, but it kept right on going.

Chris asked Pete, who was standing next to him, if he had seen anything, but Pete and everyone else had been watching other things. Chris realized he was the only one who had seen anything.

Chris rubbed his eyes again, trying to decide what to do.

CHOICE ⟹

If Chris tells someone about what he saw, turn to page 24.

Or was Chris just imagining things? If you think so, turn to page 91.

By the time they headed back to New London, the Ringers all felt like part of the *Eagle's* crew. Everyone loved the ship. She had proven able to handle anything on her shakedown cruise. With shore in sight and the real work now over, the crew was able to relax, and some of the sailors were in the mood for fun and silliness. So they introduced the Ringers to the traditional *Eagle* homecoming party. When they mentioned the word *games,* that was all it took to get the kids ready for just about anything.

Quickly, three teams were formed, and the Ringers were included on the first-year cadet team. The events were explained to them, and there was a little time to practice. Teams would compete in certain seamanship exercises, the egg drop, and a no-hands-allowed pie-eating contest.

In the seamanship events, the kids tried their best, but didn't have the experience of the sailors. Everyone, including the Ringers, got a good laugh from their efforts. The various relays involved raising certain sails, tying certain knots, and identifying various lines on the ship. The regular crew were really experts on all those and won pretty easily.

One event that the Ringers did help their team win was the life jacket relay. The idea was for the teams to have each of their members unpack, put on completely, take off, then repack a life jacket. Easier said than done!

Fortunately for the Ringers' team, their life jacket turned out to be a large size, so they were able to slip in and out of it in a hurry. During the race, straps and buckles were flying. When it was his turn, Willy yelled to the big sailor from the competing team who was struggling with his life jacket, "Is this a *life* jacket or a *strait* jacket?" Something about the way Willy said it made the sailor start laughing hilariously, and since he had the life jacket only halfway on, he got tangled up in it and fell down on the deck, where he rolled around and laughed even more—as did everyone else.

The next event was called the egg drop. The kids were all familiar with egg-toss games, but this was different. Each team sent one sailor up onto one of the spars—about forty feet above deck—with a bucket of eggs. Every teammate had a chance (and I mean *chance!*) to catch an egg dropped from that distance. Let's just say that between the Ringers, there were some omelets. Sam and Tina both managed to catch whole eggs. Willy was blinded by the sun just as his egg was dropped, and he took a direct hit on the forehead. Pete missed his egg completely, and it landed on his shoe. Jill had to catch her egg over her head, and it broke with what someone called a "scrambled shower." Jim and Chris caught their eggs—almost. They got half points for managing to keep the yolk in one piece when their eggs split in their hands.

Of course, while this was going on, there was an informal contest to establish a Guinness world record of "egg jokes." Every time an egg was broken, the entire crew yelled, in unison, "WELL, I GUESS THE YOKE'S ON YOU!" Several times, someone with a cracked egg was told, "I see you're finally coming out of your shell." One sailor's egg broke on the back of his head and ran down his shirt. That gave one of his friends a chance to ask, "Hey, Wally, if you're not a coward, how do you explain that streak of yellow down your back?" Another sailor had his egg break over his head, but the yoke stayed in one piece while the rest ran down his face. Someone yelled, "That's a message from your girlfriend, Joe. She said, 'How come you don't ever *wite* me?'" (Naturally, every attempted joke was greeted with a chorus of groans like you just made!)

After the eggs came the pies. This time, the Ringers just watched. It was wild! Five contestants from each team had to eat three cream pies apiece, using no hands. Two of the cadets managed to come in second and third in the race, which gave their team a close second place in the total games. It didn't matter. The Ringers couldn't remember a time when they'd had more fun.

That evening, the *Eagle* slowly came to her place along the pier, and the kids said teary good-byes to her and the new friends they'd made. Then the next morning, they drove by her one last time on the way out of the Coast Guard Academy. The sunrise was shining through her rigging, and she almost looked like a golden ship.

Everyone was speechless, but Sam managed to say, "If she keeps looking like that, we might have to call her the *Golden Eagle!*"

Back home, after thanks and good-byes to Lee and

Ruth Ann, the Ringers were left with enough memories to start a hundred adventure-dreams. They all decided they couldn't wait till summer, because then they were going to find a way to go sailing again!

THE END

What if those "adventure-dreams" *weren't* dreams . . . ?
Turn to page 94 and check out the other adventures the Ringers had.

Or, turn to page 121.

The pastor's direct question seemed to take the boy completely off guard. He hung his head and said slowly, "Yeah, it's been me. But I've been feeling so guilty about it, I . . . I came back, I guess. I messed up something earlier tonight and I was thinking about fixing it." He looked up. "If—if you'll let me, I'll go with you to my dad and tell him what's been going on."

Jim and Pastor Whitehead followed Charley down into the engine room. They watched him disconnect a device that he explained would have made the engine catch on fire and might have caused the fuel to explode, sending the *Niña II* to the bottom. The two Whiteheads shivered.

Afterward, they all went to the captain's cabin, where Jim Wright was fast asleep. He had some trouble waking up, but when he saw his son, his eyes shot open. "Charley? What are you doing here? I thought you'd be in California by now."

Charley began to cry.

"Dad, uhhh . . . I'm sorry I got so mad at you. I know it's not true, but . . . it felt like the ship was . . . more important to you than I was!" He paused a moment to get control of himself. "I disconected the igniter that I'd hooked up to the fuel line. If you had sailed with it on—" he wasn't sure he could say it—"the ship would probably have caught fire." He broke down again, then finally asked, "Will you forgive me?"

About halfway through his son's confession, Jim Wright had started to cry, too. He told his son that he, too, was sorry, and that the ship *had* been too important at times. "I'm sorry all this came between us. Will you forgive me too, Charley?" As the two of them hugged, Jim and his grandfather quietly left.

"They've got some fixing to do, Jim," the younger Whitehead heard the old one say as they strolled together on deck.

CHOICE

Turn to page 97.

No interesting historical visits allowed during spring break," announced Chris matter-of-factly.

The rest of the gang agreed almost instantly.

"I'm sure glad you kids aren't afraid of a little work," said Pastor Whitehead. "And if I know my friend, he'll make it worth your while."

"So, Pastor Whitehead, what are we going to do? Bust rocks or something?" asked Sam playfully.

"How many of you know what a caravel is?" asked Pastor Whitehead.

"Sure, it's what Willy piles on his ice cream," said Sam immediately.

Tina giggled and Jim tried to keep a too-straight face while he said to his sister, "Don't encourage him, Sis."

Jill said, "A caravel is an old-style sailing ship like Columbus used when he sailed to America. They have high sides and three masts."

Sam was on a roll (or so he thought). "Columbus must have read an ad in the paper that said, 'America for sale,' so he came in these ships for the sale. Get it? *Sale*-ing ships!"

Willy shook his head in exasperation. "You life be in danger, Ramirez."

"As I was saying . . . ," Pastor Whitehead cut in. He explained how his friend Jim Wright had been building a full-size copy of one of Columbus's ships, the *Niña*, to be used in celebrations commemorating the five-hundredth anniversary of Columbus's journey. "Jim will have a fine-looking ship," he said. "And believe it or not, the *Niña* was only about fifty feet long. That's not a very big ship to cross the ocean in—but we won't be doing that. Jim needs our help to put the finishing touches on her, and then we'll be giving her a shakedown cruise. What do you think?"

"What's a shakedown?" asked Tina.

"That's what they call it when they take the ship out on a trial run to make sure it does everything it's supposed to do," answered Pastor Whitehead.

Sam chimed in once more, "Well, if we work for Mr. Wright we know we can't go wrong!" With boos and hisses the rest of the gang poked at Sam.

Suddenly Willy said out of the blue, "Uh oh." The noise slowly died down.

"'Uh oh' what?" asked Sam.

"Look," began Willy, "remember what happened at school last week?"

After getting blank looks from everyone, Willy finally continued. "Remember last Tuesday when we had that career day at school? Some of you guys dared me to go visit the Coast Guard recruiter—"

"While we," interrupted Chris, "snuck off to talk to that professional football player . . . who turned out to be a third string punter? We thought we had played a trick on you, but our thing turned out to be the three *Bs*—Boring Beyond Belief."

Willy chuckled. "You know, at first I was kind of

ticked at you. But Lee, the Coast Guard guy I met, turned out to be really neat. He asked me all kinds of questions, and when I told him about the Ringers and the church, he told me he was a Christian, too. Boy, that was great! He told me he would like to visit our church and meet Pastor Whitehead sometime. I also told him about my history project, and he gave me a really awesome idea!"

Chris quickly took the floor. "Dudes and dudettes, I think we owe Willy an apology. It wasn't a very nice thing to do to leave Willy like that. I know we had a lousy time anyway, but that's no excuse for leaving a friend stranded. So, how about it?"

It took a moment for everyone to catch on that Chris was serious, and then the apologies poured out. It made Willy feel good that he could forgive his friends—and surprise them at the same time.

"So what's the 'uh oh'?" asked Pete.

Now that Willy had gotten started, he didn't know where to stop. "Lee said he could arrange for us to visit a Coast Guard ship, and probably even go out for a short cruise!"

Pete immediately asked, "Will we get to visit the radar and radio room of the ship?"

Willy shrugged. "I guess."

"I wonder if there are any girls in the Coast Guard," said Tina.

"I wonder what the food is like," said Sam, with mock disgust.

"Maybe we'll get to go on a dangerous mission and save somebody!" said Chris.

"How come you didn't tell us about all this before?" asked Tina.

"Lee asked me not to talk about it until he had checked it out."

"Sounds pretty exciting to me," piped in Pastor Whitehead. "One thing's for sure—if you're bored over spring break, it's your own fault."

"What do you think we should do, Grandpa?" asked Jim.

"It's up to you."

What will the Ringers do? It's up to you, too.

CHOICE ➡

If they go with Pastor Whitehead's plan of helping with the *Niña* replica, turn to page 106.

If they go on the Coast Guard ship, turn to page 45.

Once again, Willy was dragged away from his project. The entire gang left the Freeze with Pastor Whitehead, debating over who would get to play the part of the apostle Paul.

"I just want to be the whale!" said Sam as seriously as he could.

Willy continued the gag. "If Sam gets to be the whale, then I want to part the Red Sea so we can all walk across on dry land and not worry about the whale."

"OK," said Chris, "then I'll be Jesus sleeping in the boat during the storm!"

"And I'll be one of the disciples who threw their nets in and caught the whale," offered Jim, joining the fun.

"I'm not sure what Bible you kids have been reading," chuckled Pastor Whitehead, "but it sounds like you've got some stories mixed up. Let me set the record straight. When Paul was shipwrecked, the whales were somewhere else, the sea didn't part, and no one was fishing—at least, not in the immediate vicinity," he added with a look at Sam. "The event we will be acting out is found in Acts 27. I think we'll have Sam be Paul, and the rest of you will be Roman soldiers or crewmen on the ship."

By this time they had made their way across the Common and were entering the church. They went through those amazing doors with the beautiful carvings of a lamb and a lion, the ones that had gotten them started on exploring the mysterious old church. When they reached the place where the center aisle stopped at the front of the church, Pastor Whitehead gathered the kids around him.

"I think we'll make this as simple as possible. I want you to ad-lib the actions in the story. I'll read the story from the Bible, and you do what you think must have been happening. The altar area here will be the ship."

"Hey," burst out Sam, "I never noticed this before, but the old railing that runs here in front of the church kind of looks like the side of a ship—you know, like the Spanish galleons and stuff that you see in the old movies? Remember *Ben Hur* and the railings on the Roman boats?"

Chris cleared his throat loudly and said, "Samuel, I believe you meant to say *ships,* not *boats,* correct?"

Willy chuckled softly.

Quick-witted Sam came back: "No, Mr. Martin, I distinctly said 'boats' and that is what I meant to say. I mean, who ever heard of someone saying 'Don't rock the ship'? Everybody says 'Don't rock the boat,' right? So, I say boat!" He gave Chris a 'So there!' look that got the whole gang laughing, including Chris.

After some discussion, it was decided that Pete would be the centurion Julius, who was responsible for getting Paul to Rome, Jill would be another soldier, Willy would be the ship's captain, and Chris, Jim, and Tina would be sailors. (Sam, of course, was still Paul.) On the stage the kids found a number of cardboard boxes to set up as cargo on the ship. There were also some pieces of rope.

Pastor Whitehead read through the story while the

Ringers made up the play. Mostly they just laughed. When they were supposed to throw the cargo overboard, Paul (Sam) was almost tossed with the boxes. It took the gang a while to coordinate their movements so that it looked like they were on a ship being tossed around by the storm. But they knew they were finally getting it right when Jill shouted, "I think I'm getting seasick!"

The Pastor was pleased with their efforts, and told them they would really help the service come alive.

An hour later, Willy decided it was time to get back to work on his *Amistad* project, and Chris went with him. The group split up, promising to meet back at the church in the morning to ring the bells at eight sharp—just one of the many ways the Ringers reminded Millersburg that Jesus lived there, too.

THE END

If you want to find out the story the gang was acting out, get a Bible and read Acts 27 in the New Testament.

If you still haven't found out the story behind the ship *Amistad*, turn back to page 68 and make other choices along the way. Or, turn directly to page 50.

Chris figured he had just imagined what he saw. *I'm not used to what things look like on the water,* he thought. *And I'm not really a sailor, so I shouldn't interfere.* But then it occured to him that he should at least mention it to someone who might know better. He turned to Marley, who was standing farther up the rail. "I thought I saw someone fall off one of those sailboats when they turned around that buoy. Did you see anything?" he asked.

Marley called another sailor over who had binoculars and pointed out the area to him. The sailor panned that section of water. He stopped, seemed to double-check something, then said, "Yup, looks like we got a jetsam victim!"

"What's that?" asked Chris.

Marley smiled, and the sailor said, "Welcome to the world of lookout, kid. Sometimes we all see things at sea that turn out to be something else. Something probably did fly off the sailboat on the turn, but it's a piece of cardboard or a yellow flag. When something like this happens, you *always* gotta check it out, though, 'cause you're never sure. Thanks for mentioning it, kid—way to go. And keep up the watch!"

Marley added, "Joe here speaks from real experience. The first overboard victim he spotted for us to rescue turned out to be a dressed-up store mannequin floating in the bay. So don't ever hesitate to mention it if you think you see something while we're on patrol. We'll check it out."

Just then, the loudspeaker came to life. "Attention all hands. We have just received a distress signal off Crookes Point. A helicopter has been dispatched. We are to provide support. A yacht is sinking." Even while the announcement was being made, the *Hawk* was swinging sharply away from the Statue of Liberty and heading straight south.

"We'll be passing under the Verrazano-Narrows Bridge in a little while," said Ruth Ann. "From there it's a pretty straight shot to Crookes Point. We'll need everybody's eyes on lookout. There's no telling if the boat we're after will still be afloat by the time we get there."

In about an hour, they were on the scene. Once they had passed under the bridge, the water had gotten choppier, and the cutter rose and fell with the waves. The weather was beginning to change from sunny to stormy, and the kids could tell that the crew was worried. Because of the strong wind, the helicopter had been sent back to base. Everybody who could be spared was watching for the foundering yacht.

Pete wandered back to the command control center with Jill to watch how the radar worked. "After their SOS signal, the radio went silent," explained one of the sailors. "We're not having much luck with radar since the seas are so rough."

"Would they have had a satellite transmitter on board?" asked Pete. He knew about the way ships could be tracked by satellite if they have a special transmitter—and if someone else has a receiver to get the information from the satellite.

The sailor gave a low whistle. "Hey kid, what do you know about those?" Then he added, "But no one here is trained on our satellite receiver yet because we just got it. It's over there." He pointed to what looked like a normal radio receiver that was sitting silent in the corner.

"Mind if I look at it?" asked Pete.

"Well, just don't mess it up, kid," said the radio operator. Every few seconds he was pressing the send button on his microphone and saying, "U.S. Coast Guard cutter *Hawk* calling yacht *Marlin*. Can you respond, *Marlin?*" The only response was static.

Pete and Jill walked over to the receiver. Pete wondered if he should turn it on and try it. After all, lives were at stake. But maybe their eyes were needed up on deck, too.

CHOICE ⇒

If Pete tries using the receiver, turn to page 15.

If Pete and Jill go back on deck, turn to page 72.

With spring break coming up, who wanted to think about school? Not Chris. "OK, forget the snowball fight, Willy. But hey, listen, have you talked to the rest of the gang?" He was referring to a circle of friends in Millersburg who called themselves the Ringers. They were all the official bell-ringers at church (which was one of the reasons their gang was called the Ringers). They were always stumbling onto adventures, and had become good friends with an old minister in town, Pastor Whitehead, who was sometimes as much of a kid as they were. In fact, two of the Ringers were grandchildren of Pastor Whitehead and lived with the pastor and his wife because their parents were missionaries in Brazil.

Willy stopped. "No, why? What did they say?"

"Nothing yet. But why don't we head down to the Freeze and see if anyone else is around? Then we can all make plans together. And if no one's there, we can come back."

Willy thought for a second and then, spontaneous as usual, changed his mind. "All right." Then he added with a raised voice, "Mommm, Chris and I are going down to the Freeze for a while. Is that OK?"

"Yes," came a muffled reply.

"OK. Thanks, Mom. See you later."

"Change your clothes first!"

Willy dropped his shoulders to dramatize his disappointment at the interruption in his busy schedule. He changed into dry clothes while Chris went downstairs to his apartment and did the same. Both were soon on their way.

The Freeze was a warm place with cold ice cream. Betty Metz, the owner, used an ice-cream scoop like a magic wand. Chris, Willy, and their friends, the Ringers, used the Freeze as one of their regular meeting places. Betty loved having them around. She had even gotten dragged into some of their adventures.

When Chris and Willy arrived at the Freeze, the rest of the gang were already there, as was Pastor Whitehead. Pete, who was the tallest, was always interested in electronic gadgets. Sam, the shortest and funniest, was always trying to make someone laugh. Jill, Chris's cousin who lived in Washington, was there, too. She was staying with Chris's family since this week was her spring vacation. Jim and his shy sister, Tina, were the kids who had grown up in Brazil with their missionary family and now lived with their grandparents, Pastor and Mrs. Whitehead. The pastor and his wife had come back from Brazil to reopen the Capitol Community Church, where the Ringers had had their first adventures. Although he was old enough to be the kids' grandfather, he was like part of their gang.

"Jim's grandfather has something to ask us about spring break," said Jill.

"Us?" Chris asked. "I thought yours was almost over." As usual, he and his cousin were getting under each other's skin.

96

Tina spoke up. "Jill might be able to take an extra week off school," she explained.

"I just thought I would come back and bother you if you were doing something really fun that week," Jill added.

"So much for fun," muttered Chris under his breath.

"I heard that, you rascal!"

Pastor Whitehead cleared his throat. "I've been thinking of something we could do together when you kids have spring break. I understand from Jim and Tina that you don't have anything planned yet, and I've come up with two possibilities for you. One involves an interesting historical visit, and the other would involve several days of hard work. What do you think?"

CHOICE ⇒

What do *you* think? If the studious, eager-to-learn Ringers choose to go on the historical trip, turn to page 58.

If the adventurous, never-say-die Ringers choose to go for the hard work, turn to page 84.

The next couple of days went by quickly. Charley fit right in with the gang, working hard to clean up the ship. He knew a lot about sailing, and answered all the Ringers' many questions. And he and his dad spent a lot of time together.

Finally, the day of the *Niña II*'s maiden voyage arrived. The crew came on board early in the morning and sorted the maze of lines and sails, which had to be hung properly. They were all very efficient, and the Ringers stood back and watched in amazement.

By late in the morning the ship was ready to cast off, and so were the crew and guests. Captain Wright started the engines and moved the ship out into the Potomac River. From there, he shut down the power and ordered the sails set.

Soon they were coasting along under wind power. There were sounds, but nothing like noise—kind of like the forest at night. The kids were amazed at how quiet and almost musical it all was. The lines and the sails each had their own soft tune. And as the boat creaked softly, the water also sloshed against the hull playfully. It was relaxing and exhilarating at the same time.

They were halfway across Chesapeake Bay when the storm hit. The winds had moved up the coast faster than anticipated, and they caught the *Niña II* unexpectedly. In the few minutes of warning that they did have, Jim Wright had turned the ship around, dropped the sail, and ordered the crew to fasten everything down and prepare for a storm.

The wind, rain, and rough water hit them at almost the same time. *Niña II* was tossed like a cork. Jim Wright and his son were in the wheelhouse, struggling to maintain control of the ship. The small engine was little help. After a few minutes of fighting, Jim had his crew and Pastor Whitehead come to the wheelhouse.

Jim looked around at his rain-drenched friends and said, *"Niña II*'s maiden voyage may be her last. If the storm doesn't quit, we'll have to run her aground wherever the wind takes us. Be ready. Leonard, make sure the kids are ready, too. Everybody already has a life jacket. Show them how to clip into the safety lines on deck. Keep everyone toward the stern, but not on the castle, in case we hit something hard. We mustn't have anyone going overboard in this storm."

Near the stern of the ship there was a tarp tied down, and the Ringers gathered under it. That got them out of the rain, but most of them were so soaked it didn't make any difference. But it was also a little quieter there than out in the storm, and they huddled head to head in that protection.

It was Jim who said, "I guess we're probably all praying silently, but maybe we should also pray some out loud."

He began, "Lord, you control the wind and the rain

and the sea. You told them one day to stop and they did—on the spot. But you also let Paul go through a shipwreck and kept him safe, too. That's what we want to be: safe in your hands. In Jesus' name, Amen."

Several others prayed simple prayers. They hadn't realized until they heard his voice that Charley had snuck in with them. But now they were surprised to hear him pray, too. "Lord," he said, "it has been a long time since I talked to you. I'm not sure I ever knew you the way these guys seem to know you. But I want to trust you like they do. Please help me trust you like they do." It helped him to have the kids around him reach out and grab his hands and put an arm around his shoulders.

After a moment or two, Sam said, "Wshew! This has got to be one of the more weird places to hold a prayer meeting!" At which they all began to laugh.

They were interrupted by a shout, "Land ahead! Looks like it's probably Tangier Island. . . . We're headed for a sandbar. . . . Stand fast!"

It all happened too fast for words. Almost immediately they felt a soft scraping under the ship and she came to a sudden stop. Those who had partly risen to their feet to see what was going on were knocked down on top of the others. Then there was a surge of water behind *Niña II,* and she was driven ahead once more. But this time she didn't stop, and instead she bobbed in the water.

The forward watch shouted, "We've cleared the sandbar; we're in a calm spot. Coming ashore lightly now." Sure enough, more soft scraping, and a stop.

100

The kids heard Mr. Wright's voice. "Everyone ashore. Are all hands safe?"

Except for a few bumps and bruises, the answer was yes.

On shore, Captain Wright asked Pastor Whitehead to give a prayer of thanks, which he was glad to do.

When Pastor said "Amen," someone else suddenly started praying, and everyone bowed heads again. They all heard Charley Wright's voice say, "And Lord, thanks for my dad and for our being friends again, and thanks for these kids. They got a lot more faith than I do."

There was silence. Charley had stopped, not quite sure how to end.

"Amen," said Jim Whitehead calmly.

"Amen," echoed everyone else.

They all camped on shore that night. And the next morning the Coast Guard cutter *Hawk* towed them back up the Potomac to their home dock. The *Niña II* would sail again soon.

THE END

Turn to page 121.

Tina hesitated. She still wasn't sure they should leave the cabin, much less go outside.

Just then Ruth Ann came in. "Hi, girls! I see you're awake!" she said cheerfully. "As you've discovered, we hit some bad weather! That first blow caught us a little by surprise, but we've got the sails in now, so the wind won't affect us as much. We'll still be in for a rough ride for a while, though."

"Can we go on deck and watch the storm?" asked Jill anxiously.

"No, I'm afraid that would be too dangerous." said Ruth Ann. "Besides, there isn't much you can actually *see*. So just try and get some sleep if you can, and I'll see you in the morning."

Having to stay in the cabin wasn't as exciting as getting to be out in the storm, and so the girls soon found their tiredness returning. After a while they got used to the tilting motion of the cabin and fell asleep.

At breakfast the next morning Tina told the boys about how she had fallen from her bunk. The boys almost didn't believe it because they had slept through the entire storm!

Turn to page 78.

For once, Willy's impulsiveness gave way to good thinking. "We'll be on the ship for lunch anyway," he said. "Maybe we'll get to see more if we wait and take the tour later."

"Yeah, no sense rushing the fun part," said Sam.

"But lunch *is* the fun part!" joked Willy.

The gang decided to use their remaining time on land to explore the base, so they wandered around the chapel after the adults had filtered out. Willy, Chris, and the other guys hung around Lee while the girls tagged along with Ruth Ann. They were all poking at cracks in the walls and floor and testing the sideways movability of each and every relief they could find. This uncontrollable urge to test for secret passages required explanation, of course, but once Lee and Ruth Ann had heard the inside scoop on Capitol Community Church and the underground railroad, they understood. But the Coast Guard chapel yielded nothing. Slightly disappointed, but not really surprised, the gang regrouped to drive to the *Eagle* for lunch.

The *Eagle* was a majestic, three-masted sailing vessel as tall as a fifteen-story building and as long as a football field. Her graceful hull was pure white except for a classy-looking wide red stripe and narrow blue stripe from the deck toward the water, just back from her bow. The Ringers were speechless.

"I've got a special surprise for you," announced a crew member who met them at their van on the pier. "Captain Henry says you're invited to eat at his table!"

Now the Ringers were even more thrilled.

"Hang on to your hats, kids—he's a sharp tack!" said Lee.

"But Lee, none of us is even wearing a hat!" said Sam, breaking the mood with an attempt at humor. "What exactly do we hang on to?"

"You keep this up, Sam, and we'll end up hanging you!" said Ruth Ann, laughing.

When the captain himself welcomed them on board, the Ringers felt almost like they were in a movie. They'd seen exciting things before, but this ship was stunning! They'd never been on a deck this large or even imagined a ship this beautiful. It was a thrill just being there.

Captain Henry explained that their mini-cruise would last two or three days. "Sometimes it depends on the wind," he said. Since this was just a shakedown cruise to make sure all the work done over the winter was complete, the crew would be small, fewer than forty sailors. "And, of course, our guests," added the captain.

After their lunch with Captain Henry, Lee and Ruth Ann gave the gang a tour of the ship. They discovered they were on a floating city. The *Eagle* was home to her crew and cadets-in-training for months at a time. "There won't be time to teach you everything," said Ruth Ann, "but we hope you see some things you will want to find out more about when you go home."

At the time she said it, they happened to be standing

in the radar room, surrounded by radar screens, radios of different types—what Pete called "an electronic candy store!" His eyes shone as he looked around. He nodded at Ruth Ann's comment and said, "I already have!"

It seemed as if the gang had only begun to explore the ship when they heard the order to prepare to cast off. They stood along the railing on deck as the *Eagle* was gently tugged away from the dock and headed out to sea. The backup engines on the *Eagle* took over, and the kids watched the harbor shrink behind them.

As the *Eagle* left the harbor, the kids heard a series of commands they didn't understand, but which sent every other person on board into motion. The last command was, "Set the main!"

As the voice barked over the loudspeakers, sailors scampered up the rigging and began to release the sails that had been carefully furled to each spar (the wide crosspieces attached to the masts). The Ringers were quickly placed in two different lines of sailors who seemed ready to participate in a tug-of-war. But they weren't pulling against each other. Their ropes ran up into the sails.

"Haul!" came the command, and the Ringers found themselves right in the middle of putting a sailing ship out to sea!

For a moment, the ship looked like ten huge beds having clean sheets snapped over them. But as the wind filled the sails, they took shape and the ship surged ahead.

"They look like clouds!" whispered Jill in awe.

"Listen to the music!" said Tina, amazed by all the sounds made by the rigging, the sails, and the wind. These combined with the splashing of the waves as the *Eagle* sailed ahead.

Everyone was busy getting the ship on her way, so the Ringers wandered around and explored for the rest of the day. Mostly, they kept looking at each other as if they could hardly believe where they were!

Suddenly Lee interrupted their thoughts. "Hey, young sailors, want to join the Coast Guard?"

"Trick question, Mr. Recruiter?" asked Sam.

"Right," he replied, half ignoring Sam now that he had the Ringers' court jester pegged. "We've got spots for you kids doing lookout duty or deck swabbing. What'll it be, mates?"

The Ringers all looked at each other.

CHOICE ⇒

If the gang decides to do lookout duty, turn to page 118.

If they swab the decks, turn to page 41.

A week later, the Ringers found themselves on a dock on the Potomac River looking at the *Niña II,* a fifty-foot-long ship with a "castle" in the back. Jim Wright was proud of his work, but he also looked very tired.

"I've spent every cent I had on this project," he said. "In fact, I had to let all my helpers go because I couldn't afford to pay them anymore. That's why your help means so much." He paused. "And there's another reason too."

"What's that, Jim?" asked Pastor Whitehead.

Mr. Wright hesitated. "I hope this doesn't scare you away, but the last week or so I've been finding evidences of vandalism around here."

"Vandalism?" asked Chris.

"At first it was just tools and parts missing. But a couple of days ago I found this note stuck on the cabin door." Mr. Wright pulled a sheet of paper out of his pocket. On it were scrawled in red crayon the words, *Columbus was a bilge rat.* "I didn't know people felt that strongly about Columbus. I mean, I'm sure he didn't understand how his discoveries would change things. But I've always been amazed by his courage. Can you imagine sailing off to the edge of the world—or what everyone thought was the edge of the world—and in such a tiny ship?"

"He probably felt like I feel when I take a Social Studies test," said Sam.

"Anyway," continued Mr. Wright, "having more people around here may keep the vandals away. The police in this area haven't been too concerned. And I don't think I can stay awake another night."

It didn't take long for the Ringers to discover that the work Mr. Wright needed them to do was mostly cleaning up. The ship was really complete, and he was afraid it might be destroyed by someone before he had a chance to sail. His crew would be coming in two days to help him take the *Niña II* out for a shakedown cruise. Until then, he needed all the help he could get to clean her up and to keep her safe.

That night, when the gang gathered in the cabin of the ship for a devotional and prayer time, Pastor Whitehead organized them into three groups to keep watch: Jill, Willy, and Pete; Chris, Sam, and Tina; and Jim and himself. They all agreed each group would keep watch three hours during the night. They had prayer together, and Pastor Whitehead warned them to be careful. If they heard anything unusual, they were to awaken everyone else first, then call the police.

Jill, Willy, and Pete had the first watch—nine P.M. to midnight. Nothing happened. Their biggest discovery was that when one of them yawned, the other two got an irresistible urge to yawn also. By the time they woke up the next group at midnight, they were more than ready for bed.

For Chris, Sam, and Tina, having to wake up to do watch duty—and the fact that they were getting up at *midnight*—made things seem very different. The shadows from the lights along the dock were creepy. And although the moon was full, the sky was cloudy, so the moonlight was constantly changing and shifting as the wind blew. And there were sounds. The creaking of the ship, the lapping of the tiny waves against the pier, and the trash being blown around by the chilly wind sounded like an army of stealthy intruders sneaking up on the *Niña II*.

Staying tense requires a lot of energy, and after a while, the kids found themselves getting tired. They spoke in whispers interrupted by lengthy yawns. After a while they decided to sit on deck, back to back against the foremast while they kept watch.

One by one, they all dozed off.

Tina awoke with a start. She was sure she had heard something. Now she could hear only the soft breathing of her watchmates as they slept. She listened, but she could hear nothing.

She carefully reached around and clamped her hand over Sam's mouth. His eyes shot open and he started to struggle, but then saw Tina's finger pressed against her lips. They repeated the process with an even more startled Chris.

In a whispering huddle, Tina explained that she thought she heard something. But now all they could hear was the gentle sloshing of the water against the side of the boat.

"Are you sure you heard something?" Chris said sleepily.

"Pretty sure," said Tina, beginning to doubt herself.

Tina sighed and the three waited. Still they heard nothing unusual. What should they do?

CHOICE ⇒

If they investigate, turn to page 47.

If they decide it was nothing, turn to page 43.

Sam decided that he could put off a confession till later—maybe even indefinitely.

"I was wondering," he said, thinking fast, "will I get my hair wet?" Since he added a slight smile, the others thought he was kidding, and they laughed.

After they finished breakfast, the Ringers, along with Lee and Ruth Ann, left the *Hawk* and entered a large building on the pier. Inside was a huge pool. Ruth Ann explained that much of the water training done by the Navy and Coast Guard began in pools like this one, before the sailors were taken out to sea.

"Hey," said Willy, "this looks just like Waterworld! Can you make waves in this pool?"

"We sure can," said Lee. "And I think this will be even more fun than Waterworld!" He had the kids all change into swimsuits and put their life jackets on. Then they gathered around several rafts that were on the edge by the deep end of the pool. "These are typical survival rafts like the ones many boats and ships carry. They come with small tanks of pressurized gas that fill the raft automatically when you open the valve." He showed them. "Now things often happen quickly in an accident, so we want to teach you two things this morning. Number one is how to get into a raft like this from the water, and number two is how to control the raft in rough water. Any questions?"

Lee waited a moment, which to Sam seemed a lot longer, then said, "OK, this pool is heated, so the water will be nice. But remember that any time you go into the water outdoors, temperature will be an important factor in your survival. If you find yourself in very cold water, you will need to get into a raft quickly."

"All right," called Ruth Ann from behind them, "we've just hit a rock and our ship is sinking quickly. Willy! You and Jim push the two rafts into the pool. Everyone else, into the water. Go!"

For a moment, Sam forgot several important things: he was beside the deep end of the pool, he was afraid of water, and he hadn't buckled his life vest correctly when he put it on.

He jumped into the water with Tina, Jill, and Chris, and to his horror, he slipped right out of his life vest and headed straight for the bottom.

He was frantic as he struggled for the surface. But just as he came up, one of the rafts Willy and Jim had pushed into the water floated over him, keeping him from getting his head out of the water. He had never been so scared in his life. He tried to scream, but instead he got a mouthful of water. He looked around but couldn't think straight, and he started instinctively beating on the bottom of the raft, trying to get to air. His head began to spin.

Suddenly, an arm came around him from behind and grabbed him. He was lifted until his head cleared the water.

Sam was sputtering, coughing, and struggling when they got him to the surface. His eyes were shut. His arms were swinging wildly, and he almost slipped out of the arm that was holding him.

The air revived him and he opened his eyes. "Sam—Sam!" yelled Jill. "Stop struggling! The raft is right in front of you. Grab it!" He reached out and touched the vinyl. He lunged for it, while Jill shoved him from behind. To his surprise, he slid right up over the edge and tumbled into the raft. He was safe.

Sam's eyes cleared and he found himself looking up into Jill's smiling face as she rested her elbows over the side of the raft.

"You big lug!" she said. "Why didn't you tell us you couldn't swim?"

Sam heaved his lungs in and out, breathing in great gulps of air as the huge building echoed with his coughing and the splashing of water. Sam soon realized he was the center of attention. What he had tried to hide was now painfully obvious to everyone.

Sam felt like crying. He was ashamed for not telling the truth to begin with, but he was relieved to be alive. He shivered and said, "Thanks, Jill! You saved my life!"

"I was just the closest one to you," she said. "No big deal. Now, put this thing on right!" she added as she tossed his life vest into the raft. He put it on and double-checked everything.

"All right, everybody. Let me have your attention." It was Lee. "I'm sorry about what just happened. I should have double-checked to make sure you all knew how to swim. I guess I've got some things to learn in this job too. I'm really thankful you're OK, Sam. As long as you keep that life vest on right, you won't have any more problems with what we're learning here."

Jill added with a quick whisper, "If we have time, I'll start teaching you how to swim."

"You don't have to offer twice," mumbled Sam gratefully.

THE END

Sam did eventually learn how to swim—or at least, how to tread water. The summer he learned how to swim is another story altogether. . . .

If you haven't found out who else gets rescued, turn back to page 45 and make different choices along the way. Or, turn now to page 121.

Of course, Willy wanted to see the ship right away, so he decided to take the tour right then. Everyone piled into the van again, and Ruth Ann drove to the pier and down a lane behind some warehouses. The kids were amazed at all the different ships docked along the wharf. They got past the last building and drove into an open space. The kids all looked to their left and let out a collective gasp.

"Look at that!" whispered Willy, wide-eyed.

"I can't believe how tall those thingies are sticking up!" said Sam.

"You mean 'masts,' Sam," said Ruth Ann. "Don't call them 'thingies' or you may get thrown overboard."

"Now I know why they call them 'tall ships'!" said Pete in awe.

Lee began speaking, talking almost like a tour guide. "You're looking at the *Eagle,* pride of the U.S. Coast Guard. She's a beautiful, tall-masted sailing ship used to train officers in the ancient art of true sailing. She's two hundred and ninety-five feet long and almost one hundred and fifty feet high—that's the tallest of the three masts. But if you think this view is great, just wait until we're under full sail, with the wind making us fly." Lee paused for effect. "This will be home for the next few days!"

"It's *humongous,*" said Jill.

Sam let out a low whistle.

Jim and Tina were speechless.

"What we will be on is called a 'shakedown cruise,'" explained Ruth Ann. "The *Eagle* has been undergoing repairs and tests during the winter, and this will be her first time in the water this year. She'll be preparing to sail to Europe for a special event with tall ships from other countries. We get to make sure she's ready."

"We won't be sailing 'til tomorrow, but we can go on board now for a visit. You kids still interested?" asked Lee.

He didn't have to ask twice.

Moments later, standing on deck, the kids' awe turned to amazement at all the lines and ropes that ran from the rails up to the masts and from each sail to the mast, with even more ropes between the masts. Of course, the maze of ropes and rope ladders presented a tempting possibility.

Chris was the bold one to ask. "Can we climb up a ways?"

Lee pointed to a platform well up the mainmast. "If you're extremely careful, those who want to may climb up to that perch, but no farther."

Seven pairs of hands and feet hit the ropes about the same time. After being cooped up in a van all day the day before, it was great to be doing something energetic. It wasn't all that easy to climb the rope ladders, but a few minutes later all seven Ringers were on the observation platform about fifty feet above the deck.

Sam shouted down to Lee and Ruth Ann, "The view is magnificent!"

"Where on earth do you come up with these words like *magnificent?*" asked Chris, chuckling.

"You know, cereal boxes!" answered Sam.

After a short while, Ruth Ann reminded them it was getting to be time for lunch, so they decided to go down. Willy was the last to leave the platform, and when he looked down, he was suddenly petrified. He hadn't realized how much the height would bother him until he was up there.

"Come on, Willy," he heard Tina say, but she sounded like she was far away. Actually, she had climbed back up when she realized Willy wasn't following. Willy wasn't sure which he was more afraid of—climbing down or having the others know he was scared.

Somehow, Tina understood. She said, "Willy, have you noticed that I hardly ever talk when there are people around? I don't mind when it's just us Ringers. But I get really scared if there are other people around. If I have to speak in front of a group I freeze up."

"Well, I'm a block of ice right now," said Willy, trying to be funny.

"Look, why don't I climb down next to you, and you keep your eyes shut or just look up?" suggested Tina.

At first Willy found it embarrassing to have a girl helping him down, but then he thought to himself, *Tina is a real friend!* He also thought about the last thing the chaplain had said about making sure to take Jesus with you everywhere. *Be with me, Lord,* he prayed softly. Out loud he said, still shaking a little, "Well, I guess I have to try. Can't stay up here for the rest of my life." He got on his belly on the platform, and slid his legs over the edge and down. He hung on to the ropes for dear life.

All the way down, Tina kept talking to him. Half the time she didn't really know what she was saying. She just wanted to keep Willy's mind off his fear. About halfway down she was surprised to notice that Lee had joined them and was climbing down right next to Willy on the other side, also encouraging Willy.

When they got back on deck, Willy heaved a sigh of relief and smiled. The rest of the gang gave him a cheer. "Guess I'll have to watch how high I go climbing from now on," he said sheepishly.

"Oh, I don't know about that," answered Lee. "As long as you've got good friends around to help you, you can go just about anywhere," said Lee, giving Tina a wink. Then he added, "Hey, let's go to lunch!"

"Amen to that!" replied Willy.

THE END

Willy's challenges didn't stop there. Turn to page 102 and see what other adventures awaited him and the other Ringers.

Or, turn to page 121.

Chris was the first to speak up. "How about lookout duty, you guys? It'll be more fun than swabbing—and it'll give us a better view, too."

The Ringers didn't need much convincing.

Lee took the kids to the quartermaster, who issued each of them a pair of expensive binoculars, and the kids soon found themselves stationed along the stern (back) area of the *Eagle,* where they were to be on watch for two hours. "I know it's not exciting, but it's very important that you pay attention," Lee instructed.

The Ringers didn't need any further coaching. They recalled that at breakfast the captain had reminded the crew that the *Eagle* was a Coast Guard vessel, and that even a shakedown cruise could turn into something more if they met another craft in distress. And when the quartermaster had issued the binoculars, he said to them: "Your duties are simple: Report anything you see—*anything at all*—even if it's a piece of floating trash!"

Now, because of a storm the night before, the water was choppy.

"Having you kids keep watch will be a big help since we have such a small crew on board," Lee told them.

The Ringers all nodded.

Sam immediately challenged them all to a contest:

"First one to spot a confirmed *anything* gets something from everyone else!" The rest agreed. About that time the loudspeaker came on to notify everyone on watch that there had been a distress signal from a sailboat called *Pigeon*. The *Eagle* was on her way toward their last position.

Minutes later there came a shout from the upper lookout, "Ship sighted to port!"

Everyone looked toward the left of where the *Eagle* was headed. There, tossing wildly in the waves, was what looked like a tiny sailboat. The *Pigeon* turned out to be over forty feet long, but she was no match for the seas that day.

A sailor named Ray, who was standing next to Pete and Jim, leaned over and whispered, "Hate to ruin your fun, guys, but we have to keep a sharp lookout this way." Reluctantly, the boys turned away from the *Pigeon* and took up their watch again.

Pete's mouth dropped open as he focused his binoculars. Someone's face flashed by his sight. He looked over the binoculars and at first saw nothing, but then the waves shifted, and there, hanging on for dear life, were three people in a small raft. Ray saw it at almost the same time. He shouted, "Survivors, starboard!"

There was a flurry of activity as a lifeboat crew assembled and lowered away. In minutes, they were approaching the people on the raft. Pete watched everything through his binoculars. Chills went up and down his back. He could almost see the relief on the people's faces as each of them was helped into the lifeboat. The waves were tricky, but the Coast Guard sailors made it look easy. Ruth Ann told the kids later that the crew of the *Eagle* practice just this kind of rescue operation almost every day.

There were smiles, hugs, and cheers as the rescued people came on board. The lifeboat went back to the *Pigeon,* and several sailors stayed there to steer the boat. A line was connected between *Eagle* and *Pigeon,* as the large ship took the small one in tow. Several hours later, they met up with a tugboat, which took the *Pigeon* and her crew back to port. "All in a day's work," said Lee.

Earlier, Pete had said to Ray, his watch companion, "Thanks for reminding me to do my job. If we had kept watching the *Pigeon,* we might have missed the people!"

"We've all had to learn that one," said Ray, chuckling. "Each person's job is to make sure they watch where they're supposed to. The next time, you could be the one to spot who needs to be rescued."

"Even coming close was fun!" answered Pete.

CHOICE

Turn to page 55.

Tall ships, cutters, slavers, rescues—have you read about them all? The Ringers have seen and experienced things that will stay with them all their lives. And they've found some new interests, too. Perhaps all this will lead to further Ringer adventures.

Meanwhile, there are other things to explore: You can also learn more about the ship *Amistad* and other slavers from your library. And the Coast Guard really does have a tall sailing ship called the *Eagle* that appears in tall ship festivals all over the world. Most of the Coast Guard officers-to-be still train on this beautiful vessel.

If you've been following the Ringers for long, you know that the Bible is an important part of their adventures. For it's always an adventure trying to be a Ringer, or imitator, of Jesus.

You can find out more about the Ringers, their adventures, and how they trust in God in other Choice Adventures books.

Neil S. Wilson served for many years as a staff person with Youth For Christ and is now the pastor of Eureka United Methodist Church in Omro, Wisconsin. His writing has included curriculum for the early adolescent age group, as well as several books including *Bible Animals*, Choice Adventure #1, and portions of the *Life Application Bible*.